Super Stub

and
Other Short Stories

by
Phyllis Fraser

Andrew Benzie Books
Walnut Creek, California

Published by Andrew Benzie Books
www.andrewbenziebooks.com

Printed in the United States of America

Second Edition: November 2017

10 9 8 7 6 5 4 3 2 1

Fraser, Phyllis
Super Stub and Other Short Stories

ISBN 978-0-9852229-8-7

Cover illustration by Kassandra Robinson
Cover and book design by Andrew Benzie

TABLE OF CONTENTS

SUPER STUB
A Long Short Story

In the beginning

God walked through the Universe carrying a bucket of his newly created deoxyribonucleic acid (DNA) on his way to The Big Bang Patent Office. Nestled in the bucket were strands of this unique organic self-replicating substance, coded to implant diverse individual characteristics into living organisms. Side-stepping an asteroid, God stumbled over a small meteorite, stubbing his big toe and sending the bucket careening out into space. Clutching his throbbing foot he cried out, "Super Stub, Super Stub," while jumping up and down on the other one. Hearing the voice of God, the flying horse, Pegasus, flew down and landed beside him. Standing side-by-side, they stood silently watching the bucket bounce through the vastness of space. After 666 bounces to the 7th power the bucket landed on Planet Earth, spilling its contents all over the ground before rolling to a halt. God spoke. It was the first time the Galaxies heard the word 'Goddamn.'

There was no reason for God to go to the Patent Office now, so when Pegasus offered him a ride home, he gratefully climbed on his back. The big horse turned around, spread his wings and soon they found themselves in front of the Pearly Gates. It was not exactly the way God had planned things when he set out across the Universe, his bucket in hand four or five, more or less, billion years ago.

The dawn of man

When the bucket landed, the verdant land on Planet Earth was covered with tall trees and dense flora. Mountains and clear lakes abounded and fluffy white clouds could be seen in the blue sky. A saltwater sea contained primitive life forms, some of which would crawl on shore in the form of what would become known as beetle bugs. It was here on dry land that the dawn of man found its beginning.

God had tucked his only copy of DNA in the bucket, which he had kicked through space. When the bucket hit Earth the copy flew out and lodged in the crack in a stone, an ancient stone destined to be used as part of the Wailing Wall in Jerusalem after mankind had evolved and divided into great civilizations. Over countless stretches of time so many wet salty tears would be shed by men on this wall that the only legible writing remaining on the stone, when it was found, were the letters D, N, and A. The scholar, Rabbi Maimonides, would proclaim the letters God-sent and declare their meaning to be Do Not Ask. So nobody did. He was guessing, but nobody thought to ask about that either.

Back to the beginning

When the bucket landed on Earth a looooong time ago, the only animal protoplasm on the planet was in tiny beetles, identical copies of each other. These organisms never felt a need to be different, go anywhere, or even vary their diet. (Thousands of years later a few of these beetles would be discovered under rocks or ice having left their crispy little bodies for paleontologists to study.) Soon after the bucket collided with Earth the beetles began absorbing its contents, which caused their bodies to mutate into higher life forms and pass these changes to their progeny, a process known as Evolution. Finally, with the advent of human life, about 400 million years later, Homo-Sapiens (modern man) acquired the ability to stand upright, form thoughts, speak words, and learn to make choices. In time, they gathered together in diverse groups to start exploring their surroundings, eventually claiming ownership and control of the entire planet. God could neither change the past nor the glut of good or evil that would follow in its footsteps.

Thus, began man's future. Jealousy, war, greed, boundary disputes, taxation, government graft, slaughter of the animals, demolition of the forests; and finally weapons of mass destruction would plague the development of civilization. It was just about all God could stand. But, on the other hand, he saw love, happiness, tenderness, kindness, the arts, music, literature, as well as the theater develop and his heart filled with compassion.

As it was in the Beginning it is now and ever Shall Be

The human soul is often thought of as conscience, but this is not so. Conscience is the knowledge of right and wrong with an inner urging to do right. It is the soul that makes this choice. Each person has a soul, an indefinable, invisible, but eternal spiritual reproduction of himself containing the quintessence of his beliefs.

But again, back to the beginning, this time behind the Pearly Gates.

It was during an Eclipse of the sun and Earth about the time Homo Sapiens started out on their earthly journeys into their future that God rose to his full height and smote his forehead with an open palm. Immediately, a constellation of brilliant colored stars lit up the night sky. It was the first Aurora Borealis seen on Earth and it was in that moment, God's home became both Heaven and Hell. The Pearly Gates instantly turned into turnstiles to welcome souls of the dead with four rules posted over each entrance.

1. No Soliciting
2. No Weapons
3. No Money
4. No child left behind.

It is deserving of our attention to remember that turnstiles move only in one direction. Once inside, there is no choice but to greet an Eternity that will mete out just rewards for the choices made on earth. And so, it is and ever shall be. God rested.

And I shall dwell in the house of the Lord Forever

A difficult concept for an outsider to imagine is Time behind the turnstiles. There isn't any. Time, known to man on earth as linear, remains, but a memory for the occupants in the afterlife. However, God still programs their daily living to a 24-hour day for the sake of their sanity. Space becomes timeless; it's like picking up encyclopedias with characters moving in random throughout the pages. You may meet Socrates speaking softly to Freud and Jung, or Hitler and Robespierre out-shouting each other, or Shakespeare and Thespis with their heads together, or a Stone Age party of cave dwellers hunched around a warm incandescent fire watching a Marilyn Monroe movie. But back to existence or, if you so choose, nonexistence beyond the turnstiles.

The fables of Heaven being Up and Hell Down are quite untrue. There are 3,000 stairs leading up to Hell. Heaven takes place on the ground floor. Heaven becomes, to each tenant, exactly as he imagined it. All occupants of both floors now think of Earth as their birth mother and God their father and Eternity their home. This pleases God immensely.

Both Heaven and Hell abound with humans in various stages of development. Paintings adorn the corridors of all the buildings. Babies and children all dwell only on the bottom floor. Children laugh and play together in unbridled freedom in an open-air park as music softly plays in the distance.

Discussion groups held in Heaven are continually surprised by the diverse souls who enter into their midst. Through the centuries, separate rooms have been cordoned off, adjacent to the auditorium to honor the great philosophers, who still aren't sure where they are, Christian Scientists who know they are not here, and Agnostics who discuss if they are here, there, or anywhere.

Upstairs, those in Hell must rotate their work and come downstairs three times a day with a prepared variety of gourmet foods to serve the occupants of Heaven. Then, after cleaning up, they immediately return up to Hell carrying the leftovers for the occupants of the upstairs.

With these routine chores and their constant maneuvering from one floor to the other, it is exhausting for the upstairs group so they have little energy left to pursue their own interests.

No children, animals or birds are seen in Hell. The pictures along Hell's corridors depict swords, guns, tanks and famous prison camps. Clocks with no faces and sirens blowing at random are placed behind barbed wire fences in the execution gardens. God, not unkind, sees enough chaos on Earth to grant the residents in Perdition with familiar surroundings, very similar to those they created on earth.

For atheists, the upstairs holds an expanding windowless wing, housing an empty workshop with seats on the floor, for souls doing nothing—conscious only of the dark emptiness, a void that will gradually absorb them into nothingness. They sit complacent in the knowledge that their thinking is accurate.

*   *   *

It started out like any other pseudo morning in eternity, but would soon change when an unexpected darkness descended with a bang. God, reading the Star Bulletin under the bright skylight in the Atrium, looked up. The sky outside had turned into a giant swirling black funnel, pulling everything in its path into its depths, clouds, stars, meteorites even Heaven and Hell and the 3,000 stairs between them flew up through the skylight in less than a nanosecond. The noise was unbearable like the suction of a mighty drain. The Pearly Gates and turnstiles were no longer standing. People, cows, architecture all imploded as they were pulled into the dense gravity of a passing black hole. God, gripping a hot cup of Starbuck's decaffeinated cappuccino, found he was being sucked up into the hole. Then, before he knew it, he found himself standing alone on solid ground at the other end of the funnel.

It was quiet, much too quiet. No birds or beasts were in sight. Only the music of the spheres played softly. Majestic mountains stood in the distance, soft sunlight filtered through the green trees and a lake lay blue and clear not far from where he stood. Only a single white cloud floated in a tranquil sky.

After perusing these surroundings God looked down at the ground and saw a slight movement next to his foot. Bending over for a closer look he saw a few tiny beetles, all walking straight ahead. Holding his coffee securely in both hands, he took a sip through the little hole in its plastic cover as he mused, then smiled, and thought,

Perhaps they will be better off this time around if I don't kick the bucket.

After God finished his coffee, Pegasus flew down and landed beside him. For just a second, God looked over and thought he saw the horse smile.

Divine Wind

It was late afternoon when the sunny day suddenly flipped to the other side of the coin. Outside, the tall cane stalks bent and whipped in the wind as rain came down in torrents. December in Hawaii is the rainy season. The red earth outside turned to mud and the grey clouds blotted out any blue sky. When the electricity failed, she lit a kerosene lantern, placed it on the kitchen table, and picked up the telephone. There was no dial tone. Helen was home alone.

She had been through these island storms before, but never without Jed. After placing her elbows on the table, she cupped her chin in her hands. She knew there was nothing to do but wait it out. Evening was approaching so after a few minutes she stood up, poured a glass of wine, sipped it slowly and listened as the wind weakened. Realizing she was hungry she opted for a cold chicken leg and a ripe mango, which she ate in the eerie light from the lantern, her skin damp and shiny from the humidity. Soon the sunset came and by nightfall the storm had abated and stillness had taken its place.

*   *   *

Helen and Jed Henderson lived on the Island of Kauai in a tiny wooden house originally built sometime in the mid 1930s as a residence for a local sugar plantation supervisor. This little house, owned and rented to them by a Japanese couple, stood isolated at the end of a dirt road running into a sugarcane field. Their only neighbors were a utility pole located about a half a mile from the junction of their driveway and the main highway, and a shack another half a mile further down on the beach. The closest town was Waimea, six miles to the west, and like most small Hawaiian towns, it consisted of only a bank, dry goods store, grocery store, police station, and a dispensary.

Knowing she must work the next day, Helen got ready for bed, where she curled up and slept until about two in the morning, awakening with what sounded like a car door shutting. Hoping it was Jed she raised her head from the pillow to listen but heard nothing further. The electricity was still off, the rain had stopped, and a full moon shown through the window. Wide-awake she went to the kitchen, poured herself a glass of water, smoked a cigarette and then went back to bed. Helen never worried about her husband, as he had lived in Indonesia, navigated the Pacific and survived in many a storm, but still she would have felt better if he were home. Unable to go back to sleep she got up, dressed in her uniform and sat down at the kitchen table waiting for Jed, who arrived at sunrise, exhausted muddy and wet after trudging through the cane fields. He had opted to stay in a nearby cave during the night, as the Menehune Ditch was too flooded to wade across. After giving Helen a quick peck on the cheek he headed for the shower where he let out a four-letter expletive upon discovering the water was cold. Wrapping a towel around his waist he headed for the kitchen where he sat down to a bowl of cold cereal before making his way into their bedroom for a few hours' sleep.

*   *   *

Helen worked as a nurse at the Waimea dispensary. It was morning, the air hung humid and heavy and the cane stalks in the field outside once again stood still and upright. She grabbed her purse and walked to the carport. After sliding behind the wheel of the car she caught her breath when she turned to put her purse on the backseat. A young man was stretched out across the seat his mouth open and his eyes bulging, his body cold to her touch. She remembered that moment in the night when she thought she heard a car door slam.

Leaping out of the car she ran into the house calling Jed's name. She remembered a rooster crowing just seconds before Jed sat up with a start, jumped out of bed and followed her to the car. After looking at the boy in the backseat, they went inside to call the police but the phone was still out so they agreed to drive into Waimea together. Jed put on an aloha shirt and shorts and Helen sat next to him in her starched white nurses uniform, both silent on the short drive.

As the police station was next door to the dispensary, Helen and the chief had a nodding acquaintance. Helen went in the station and explained the situation to Chief Keoke who soon returned with two policemen who took the body out of the car and into the morgue, a small building behind the dispensary. As the men lifted the body from the backseat Helen took a closer look at the young Caucasian probably in his late teens. He had been strangled. It was not a pretty sight.

The Henderson's followed Keoke into the station and Chief invited Helen to use the wall phone to call in late to the dispensary.

The police station looked like a building out of a western movie. An old rickety veranda that creaked with every step, ran across the front of the building. The weather-beaten building had small windows on either side of a wooden door with the key still in its rusty lock. Inside, mismatching wood and rattan chairs were placed at random around wooden tables. Everything was tinged with years of red dirt. The walls, floors and even the ceiling were a monotone of the prevalent earth color. A door on the back wall led to the chief's office. The printing on the door said Private.

Chief Keoke, a corpulent man of pure Hawaiian descent, beckoned them back to his private office where he sat down behind his desk. As there was only one chair facing him he offered it to Helen.

"Sit down please Mrs. Henderson. Mr. Henderson please bring in another chair from the waiting room."

When Jed returned with a rattan chair and was seated next to Helen, the chief looked at both of them. "Did either of you recognize the boy in your car?"

Jed denied ever having seen him but Helen thought for a minute as she looked down at the floor then out the window and across the desk before she met the Chiefs eyes, "No, Chief I know I've never seen him before in my life."

"Think again—are you sure?"

Keoke looked at her quizzically, then hesitated before continuing, "Didn't I see him with your husband?"

She shrugged her shoulders. "I already told you I don't know who he is?"

She realized she was sounding irate and impatient as she thought of the patients piling up in the dispensary, so tried to speak more gently, or as Jed would have said, to soft-pedal her replies. "Like I told you, I just found him in my car this morning, woke Jed and we drove directly here. I'm really sorry that's all I can tell you."

The chief hesitated as he studied Jed's face. "His driver's license says he is from California. He might have been nosing around the Menehune Ditch. Maybe you know him Mr. Henderson?"

Helen spoke up before Jed could answer, "What do you mean nosing and why are you looking at Jed like that?"

Helen spoke in a more agitated tone than she intended realizing how tired she really was. Hoping to end the interview she stood up, almost tripping over a box of fishing nets on the floor beside her, but kept her eyes on the Chief until he answered.

"Because he had a paper with your phone number clutched in his hand, and because you said you didn't know him. Why didn't you ask me if I knew his name? Is there something wrong, something you aren't telling me?"

"Chief Keoke, I didn't know him, please believe me! I have told you all we know, now I should really get over to the dispensary, as Dr. Brenecke has a tonsillectomy scheduled in ten minutes." Walking out the office door she heard Keoke's next question but not Jed's answer.

"Mr. Henderson, tell me what you know about this boy again?"

The Chief took Jed into the morgue for another look at the body but Jed denied having known or ever having seen the boy. Keoke then let him go home.

*   *   *

That evening even though the storm was over and the sultry stillness seemed almost stifling, it was their interview at the police station that left the Henderson's most uncomfortable. When they arrived home the electricity was back on and the telephone was in working order. Helen prepared a salad in the kitchen and Jed studied his charcoal rubbings, but both were really thinking of the body in the morgue. They spoke little at dinner except to say how mystified they were about the murder and how tired they were of the changeable weather. Jed lit a cigarette before he went back to the rubbings.

After washing the dishes Helen put on her pajamas and got into bed with a book. Her mind skipped back five years to the time when they moved from California to Honolulu, and Jed enrolled at the University of Hawaii, studying to become an anthropologist. In order to help with expenses, she got a job as a nurse at Queens Hospital across town from the University.

After Jed received his Master's Degree, they left Honolulu and moved to the Island of Kauai where he was now working toward a doctorate studying Hawaiian petroglyphs found on Kauai, dating back a thousand years; picture graphs possibly able to shed light on the odyssey of the ancient Polynesians. The Hawaiians had a legend that the fishpond outside of Waimea had been built overnight by a race of tiny people called the Menehunes, who then disappeared, never to be seen again. A scattering of stones of unknown etiology carved with primitive stick-like figures were part of the construction of this fresh water fishpond, known locally as the Menehune Ditch. Renting a little house in the cane field very close to the site, Jed carefully took rubbings as well as photographs of the carvings on the stones.

Later when he slipped into bed beside her, the trauma of the past day eased as she snuggled into his protective arms. Soon both fell into a dreamless sleep.

*   *   *

The following afternoon Helen stayed late at the hospital to assist in the difficult birth of a 13 pound Hawaiian baby and upon arriving home opened the door, turned on the lamp and looked around aghast. There were papers strewn all over the floor, but what was really frightening was the scene at the dining room table.

All day Jed had been among the rocks along the Menehune ditch and he walked in just moments later to find her staring as motionless as a statue at a young man his head thrown back both eyes open and his tongue blue and bulging from his open mouth.

Helen lifted her hands to her mouth before she dropped them to her side and spoke. "My God Jed, look!! Just like the other one." She turned to look at her husband, now a pasty white as he gripped the back of a dining room chair and stared at the boy.

Chief Keoke was summoned and arrived within minutes. After being assured by the Henderson's that they did not know this boy and ascertaining nothing had been stolen Keoke had no choice but to call the station for assistance to transport the body to the morgue.

Helen straightened up the papers strewn around the room. Jed made a pretense of working. Helen felt ill at ease, as she had seen a look of doubt come over Keoke's face when they both adamantly denied knowing the young man, but they had no answer other than the truth.

*   *   *

The next day the second boy was identified as a 19-year old student from Arizona attending the Univ. of Hawaii. In Honolulu Dr. Palmer in the Anthropology department was apprised of the situation and verified both boys had been undergraduate students.

In the evening, Helen cooked an early supper of fried rice, chicken and pineapple but neither ate much as they mulled over the murders. Two students from the mainland each killed and both students at the U. of H. It didn't make any sense, especially the young man in the car, found clutching their phone number and address. Why? Until now their life was idyllic. A Polynesian paradise was rapidly turning sour.

Masa, a 17-year old Hawaiian boy, lived in the shack on the beach within walking distance of the Henderson's. Helen knew him from the dispensary, where he had been recently seen for coral cuts on his feet. There was no reason for Keoke to question him, but Helen thought of another angle right after supper. Even though it was getting dark, she walked down the muddy dirt road to the oceanfront, and knocked on Masa's door. He invited her in, and when she told him the reason for her visit he thought for a minute before he answered.

"No Mrs. Helen, I no see no haolies (Caucasians) near you house, you got pilikea (trouble)? Something missing? Funny you ask? My sampan been stay missing since the storm. I figure it wash out to sea but that no ever happen before. I always plenty careful to tie it high up the beach. Hmm?"

Remembering the legend of Madam Pele, ancient goddess of the volcano who supposedly could be seen sometimes walking at night, Helen said, "I don't know Masa, maybe Madam Pele went for a ride." A weak answer but it did make him laugh.

At that same moment, Helen glanced over at the open window to see a pair of hands loosen their grip on the sill. There followed a soft thud as a body hit the sand. Someone had been watching them.

Walking home the full moon lent its bright light to the path and she walked slowly along until a pebble in her shoe caused such pain she had to sit down under a tree and take the shoe off. It was then that she heard voices coming from the other side of the tree. The trunk was thick and the branches heavy with large green leaves reaching the ground so there was no worry about being seen and apparently the man and woman had no worry about being heard for they were talking in normal tones, audible over the lapping surf. A large cloud moved over the moon shrouding the area in almost complete darkness. She hunched over with her arms wrapped around her knees as she listened. The man cleared his throat and spit before he spoke.

"Yes, I looked in the window and could hear, but they were talking about Madam Pele. I don't think…"

The woman interrupted with a sigh of relief and in an impatient voice took over the conversation.

"Number one OK, now it's all set. We'll put the boxes in the shed, and tell Mrs. Henderson, if she asks, that it's clothing to send our relatives in Japan. That husband does nothing but dig around Menehune Ditch anyway so he'll not bother. We are lucky they have no children."

Helen held her breath as she listened to her landlord and his wife, the Matsumoto's. Tseuto worked at first Hawaiian Bank across from the Waimea police station, and his wife Eureko ran the grocery store next door.

They stood up and walked toward the ocean, still speaking but soon out of sight and sound. What Helen did not hear were the next words Eureko said to Tseuto.

"Are you sure the boys didn't see Mr. Jed after they left the bank?" and he replied.

"No I kept watching them, they didn't see anyone, talk to anyone, or get out of my sight." Then turning to Eureko he gave a little laugh before continuing.

"Don't worry Eureko San, nothing will throw any suspicion on us. Yoko San will meet us in Honolulu as planned. I took care of everything." He spit in the ocean. The incoming tide erased their footprints along the shore.

Later that evening when the Matsumoto's put the boxes in the shed, they didn't see Helen crouching in the darkness behind the fertilizer bags. Without speaking they left. When Helen was sure they had gone, she opened one of the big boxes to find a number of smaller boxes inside. Opening one of the little boxes she closed it quickly, hiding it behind a shovel leaning against the wall. Then she opened the shed door a crack and looked out into the moonlight to make sure nobody was in the yard before she crept back to the house. It was well after midnight but Jed was still hunkered down over his desk.

He looked up, when she tapped him on the shoulder, "I know it's late darling but just one more rubbing."

"Jed listen to me. This really can't wait. The Matsumoto's are putting boxes of money in our shed." Then she told him about hearing plans to send the boxes to Honolulu.

"Whoa there Helen hold on, you mean Tseuto, but why?"

"I don't know Jed, maybe he robbed the bank. Perhaps they put those boys on our property and the money in our shed, so in case they got caught they could blame it on the boys and us. I just bet those kids saw something the Matsumoto's didn't want them to see."

But why all the money? I just don't get it Helen." Jed gathered the rubbings into a pile. "How many boxes are there?"

"I don't know exactly and am afraid to look tonight as they might see me. I took one small box and hid it by the door. Let's go to bed it's nearly midnight. We can look in the morning."

*   *   *

On December 5th, an article appeared in the Kauai Island newspaper. A house belonging to the Matsumoto's of Waimea, and rented to a student from the University of Hawaii and his wife, burned to the ground just after midnight, the morning of December 5th, taking the lives of the young student and his wife. The owners of the house, Tseuto and Eureko Matsumoto, could not be found and may have also perished in the fire. Only a gardening shed adjacent to the house escaped the blaze. A small box of paper money was found in the shed, the serial numbers matching those on the bills reported missing last week from the first Hawaiian Bank in Waimea.

On December 6th, Chief Keoke told his wife it was undoubtedly by mistake that the Henderson's left the box of money behind. There were tracks in the dirt outside the shed like heavy objects had recently been pulled over the ground. Probably, the Henderson's had dragged the rest of the bank's missing money inside their house.

After thinking a moment, the Chief continued, "My theory is that the boys were paid to rob the bank, having been promised a cut, and were killed when they delivered it. Why else would the Henderson's phone number be in the boy's hand? There was no sign of arson. The fire destroying the house was probably started by a cigarette—both the Henderson's were heavy smokers.

Keoke, a God-fearing man, bowed his head in silence, convinced his explanation was an irrefutable truth. Nodding his head, he tenderly reached out and took his wife by the hand. "You know, my manu-aloha (love bird), that nurse just acted too darned nervous when I questioned her. I thought at the time something was wrong. We must remember that God gives out justice in His own way and it is not up to us to judge."

Leoni looked into her husband's eyes. "Keoke you be one smart Hawaiian."

*   *   *

A sampan bobbed in the blue waters off Waikiki early in the morning of Dec 7th, 1941 as Kamikaze pilots flew over Pearl Harbor, Hawaii, dropping bombs on the American fleet below. Tseuto looked up just in time to see a bomb falling straight for their sampan, but it was too late. In the next second Eureko, Tseuto and over a million dollars in cash blew up into thousands of pieces. This may have been the smallest boat ever sunk by the enemy in what was to become a long and costly war.

Thoughts

Morning

It was 9 o'clock in the morning. It seemed like everything in the house demanded my immediate attention; Billy cried, the doorbell chimed, Molly barked, the phone rang and adding to this turmoil the timer buzzed. Whirling like a dervish, I set priorities. I picked up Billy, shooed Molly out the back door, then trotted back to the kitchen and turned off both the timer and the stove on my way to the front door. The telephone on the kitchen wall had stopped ringing before I could answer it, but the doorbell continued chiming its monotonous two-bell ring. Reaching the door I knew before I opened it she would be standing there.

I stood for a minute with my hand on the doorknob arranging my mouth in a smile before opening the door to my mother-in-law, her index finger aiming in the air straight for another jab at the bell. Drawing her hand back, her brow knitted in a patronizing look, she tilted her head in a position of exaggerated concern before speaking.

"I thought you would never answer. Where were you Doreen? Were you not up yet?"

I looked down at my soiled apron. I wasn't wearing any makeup and Billy had reached up and pulled a strand of my uncombed hair over my face, which added the final touch to my al la frowsy housewife look. After tucking my hair back in place I shifted Billy to the other hip.

I wondered why she had to come so early in the morning—she could call me first. I'd never looked worse. Come on Janice, couldn't you hold off for just an hour? Let me brush my hair or make my bed or better yet hide in the front closet? I really don't need your input today. I can't possibly match your silly smile so I won't even try.

But I said, "I'm just fine, Janice, come on in."

As usual Janice could have stepped out of Harper's Bazaar. Simply everything matched, even the lipstick and Christian Dior shoes. She walked gingerly down the hall like she was afraid of stepping in something soft and slippery and once in the living room brushed off the sofa of any possible toys, dirt or contaminants before sitting down.

I thought, no darn it—I'm not fine and that sofa is not harboring the bubonic plague, so just quit looking around the room like it should be on some TV makeover show.

After placing Billie in the little swing seat next to his grandmother and handing him a rattle I said, "I'll just go comb my hair and put on a little lipstick, be right back."

When I came back from the bedroom Molly, our tiny white Westie terrier had started to bark, so I let her inside. She immediately jumped on Janice, her sharp claws catching her skirt with each lunge. Janice treated her with distain pushing her down and screaming, "No, no, little dog!"

"I thought I've told you a million times—why couldn't you just say, 'down Molly?' She thinks you're playing. The dog has a name, in case you've forgotten—it's Molly. Besides if you just said 'down' she obeys . . . well, sometimes."

I grabbed Molly by the collar and led her back outside, then went to the kitchen and poured the water off some very hardboiled eggs before returning to sit next to Janice on the couch. Janice said something about the weather at the same time Billy started to cry. He was hungry. After lifting him out of his little swing, I sat down on the couch and unbuttoned my blouse while Janice averted her eyes to the watercolor on the wall.

I thought, *excuse me your majesty.* I usually just take him to the wet nurse in the adjoining castle where three ladies in waiting are poised with gossamer designer gowns and matching slippers for me to choose my breakfast while Billy dines and the prince awaits my whims,

Then, she interrupted my fantasy, which was beginning to sound pretty good. "Why, oh why are you still nursing that child? I stopped nursing my son when he was two months old. It might leave you more time for your chores dear."

After a slow critical perusal of the room she nodded her head from side-to-side and geared her voice to that poor-thing-I pity-you benevolent tone, she is so fond of using on me. "Really young lady, I think maybe that dog is too much for you to care for right now. Dogs can take up so much of one's time."

I wanted to say you really take up more of my time than that dog ever has. I decided not to go there. "Must you always refer to Molly as "that dog" and James as "my son" and Billy as "that child?" They all have names.

But instead I said, "The doctor says breast milk is good and I have plenty and . . ."

Janice interrupted, "Oh, times have changed since I had a baby."

I chose not to be pulled into that one either, so we sat quietly for a minute. Billy was soon satisfied and sleeping so I asked, "Would you like a cup of coffee?"

The telephone rang before she could answer, so excusing myself and still holding Billy I went to the kitchen.

"Hello?"

"Honey is that you? Are you OK I tried to get you earlier?"

"I'm fine James. Your mother is here and we are having a little chat."

As Janice couldn't see me in the kitchen from her position on the couch I took this opportunity to stick my tongue out at her. It felt good, so good that I did it again.

Then with my tongue once again back inside my mouth I said, "Just let me put Billy down. Be right back."

With Billy sleeping in his crib I returned to the phone, "OK, James I'm here what were you were saying?"

"Give my mother my love. Do you think you could accommodate Mr. McDonald and Mrs. Zweisman, a new advertising director the firm is considering hiring, for a home-cooked dinner tonight? Mrs. Zweisman has been on the road for a week and was saying after our morning meeting that she was so tired of restaurant meals. Might be just the thing to turn her head in our direction? OK? Just cook something simple. Maybe a down home type of soup or whatever's easy?"

I gulped before answering, "Sure honey, say around 7, cocktails first?"

Mr. McDonald was the vice president—I have always been a little scared of him—and this woman, I don't even know her! She could be Jewish so I can't have roast pork like I had planned, and the house is a mess and Billy is teething so how do I get everything ready on time?

Janice was leaning forward on the couch trying to catch the gist of our conversation, so returning to the sofa, I simply told her James was bringing Mr. McDonald and some business associate over for dinner tonight and I would have to get things ready.

"That is so nice of you dear. Try to make time to get your hair done and I noticed the front porch needs sweeping. A first impression is a lasting one you know?" She gave a little chuckle as she held her hands out in front of her, inspecting her perfectly manicured fingernails before she smiled and looked up at me.

I answered her by simply walking to the kitchen saying, "Let's have our coffee now."

I poured her a cup and while handing it to her I smiled.

Screw you lady—can't you get your own coffee? You could offer to help with something other than criticism. Never once have I seen you behind a broom, mop, or in front of a stove let alone sweeping a front porch. Sure, I'll just get my hair done while Mary Poppins does the rest.

The morning went by with the usual chitchat and helpful suggestions to improve my endeavors in the kitchen and dining room. She never had any hints for the bedroom and for that I was thankful. She also did not gossip about people, which could have been a real downer.

I thought of her as our lady of unsolicited suggestions, criticism, and censure. I knew little about her family, childhood, or schools or if she had ever read a book. I did ask her once and she said her family was from the old country, Wales, and then immediately changed the subject. No, Janice visited me on her own terms, lock, stock and barrel, subject, verb and predicate.

Noon

Billy was awake and fussing, so I picked him up, knowing better than to ask Janice to help with 'that baby.'

Never once had she asked to hold her grandson except at his baptism when she posed with him in her arms beside the baptismal font as motherly as the Virgin Mary. But that was six months ago. And after all she was having her picture taken.

From my vantage place on the couch I took inventory of the living room, estimating the time it would take to make it presentable. Janice interrupted my visual perusal.

"What are you having for dinner? Don't make lasagna—it was a little dry last time. Safeway makes a good lemon pie. I think you should take the toys and that dog bone out of the living room before they get here.

I turned to her and used the four words that would always stop her, "You are right Janice." She would never argue with that bit of wisdom.

I thought to myself, Janice, I don't know what I want for dinner—just let me sit here a minute. I have sense enough to take the crap, including you, out of the living room, but give me a chance to decide what to cook and really Janice just go home. There is nothing wrong with my lemon pie, I notice you always eat every crumb.

Then it came to me that while I wasn't the dullest knife in the drawer I wasn't the sharpest either, or I wouldn't let her get to me.

I offered her a second cup of coffee and some cookies before I started to pick up Billy's toys. She accepted the coffee and went to the refrigerator helping herself to a bowl of tapioca pudding while saying something about it being lunchtime before continuing on her monotonous diatribe. I only halfway listened as I picked up the familiar theme of her monologue along with the familiar toys around the room.

"I think you should wear a white blouse and just a touch of makeup around your eyes so you won't look so tired. I am glad to see you are letting your hair grow a little longer. You are such an attractive girl, you should really take better care of yourself." Then she left the couch and put her empty pudding dish in the sink before returning to the couch.

I invited her to stay for a simple lunch, she accepted and we both had turkey sandwiches and sliced pineapple. I straightened up the kitchen, and then it was time to feed Billy.

It was nearly two o'clock before she left—waving a final farewell, before throwing a gem of parting wisdom over her shoulder as her designer heels clicked down the walkway, "Don't forget to sweep the front porch."

I thought to myself, Janice see that drain at the end of the driveway just keep walking right straight into it. The cover is loose.

Instead I heard myself say, "Watch out for the drain at the end of the driveway, I think the cover is loose," wondering why I warned her, but not really wanting to see anybody so well dressed in the sewer, I waved a friendly good-bye.

The afternoon slipped away as I finished cleaning the house. I cooked orange honey chicken thighs with sesame topping, made a tossed green salad and thawed a chocolate cake, then set the table with the good china.

Showering and changing into a white pants suit and slipping on my white sandals I put some makeup under my eyes, for upon close scrutiny I did look tired. The clock said I had fifteen minutes until the chicken would be done and James would be due to come home. Putting Molly and her bone outside, I prayed she wouldn't bark throughout dinner. Billy was sleeping in his crib and all was ready just before I heard footsteps coming up the walkway.

Night

The door opened, James and the guests walked into the house and down the hall to the living room. After meeting Mrs.

Zweisman and the usual amenities were finished, James made the drinks.

I wanted to say, 'nice to meet you too, I wish the evening were over. Thank God Billy is sleeping and James is such a good host.'

Instead, I said, "I am so happy to meet you, Mrs. Zweisman and to see you again. Mr. McDonald. Please do sit down and make yourselves at home."

Everyone had cocktails, and I passed the chips, dip and plate of crackers and cheeses. After the second cocktail, Mrs. Zweisman insisted on being called Elsie. Mr. McDonald was interested to learn we had a Westie Terrier and told me all about the one his brother had in Scotland, called Tartan and asked to meet Molly.

Dinner went well until Billy cried and I had to leave the table, but I did return in time to serve the coffee and dessert. Elsie, a tall thin business-like woman, just this side of fifty and the other side of pretty, wore her dyed-black hair twisted in a knot on the nape of her neck. Mr. McDonald, a widower of many years, seemed fascinated with her, although she was a good five inches taller than he. When she asked to see Billy I was delighted, and when she asked to hold Billy even more so. She told me she was the oldest of eight children and loved taking care of babies. I could have kissed her but I didn't, we just talked about the joys of holding a baby in your arms. I wished she had been here this morning.

A relaxed demeanor, a ready smile and Clark Gable's good looks under a shock of prematurely grey hair was the best way to describe James. After the usual polite exchange of departing words of appreciation and thanks, James walked the guests to their cars, waving as they pulled out of the driveway. I was so proud of my husband.. James turned to me and let out a sigh of relief after he came back in the house.

"Thanks honey, that was a good dinner. Don't you like Mrs. Zweisman, I mean Elsie? She seemed to be enjoying herself. The old girl took immediately to Billy and Molly. I think McDonald has his eye on her. Hope so." Singing a verse of *Old McDonald*

Had a Farm, he danced twice around the kitchen table before he helped me clear the dining room table.

It had been a relatively early evening as everybody had to work the next day. In the kitchen James put his arm around my shoulders as he said, "Doreen we have to get the drain fixed at the end of the driveway. The cover is loose and somebody might fall or catch a heel in the grating. Will you call the city in the morning? Thanks darling."

I thought maybe the repair crew wouldn't get here before Janice. I knew I was only kidding, and told myself that was not even near a kind thought—but I did smile when I thought of one of Janice's Christian Dior shoes wedged in the grating. Perhaps she would be trapped all morning. She might just stand there until the city repair crew found her. James was watching me as I smiled at this thought.

"Honestly, Doreen good to see you smile. I am so pooped, I envy you able to relax at home in peace and quiet and sip tea with my mom. It's nice for Mom, she never had many friends. Sure must be great not to be on a deadline. Billy was so good tonight. You don't look tired so why don't you stay up and watch TV if you'd like. I simply have to hit the sack." Then after kissing me goodnight he marched up the stairs.

I began loading the dishwasher and thought back over the day with his mother.

Janice, are you lonely? Maybe that's why you come across so bossy. You have no idea how you come off, you really don't. You hesitate to court either the love of that child or even that dog. Could that be why you don't give them names? Maybe things starting with capital letters, things breathing, if unnamed can't hurt you. Are you afraid of rejection? That son of yours said his father left you before he was born. Did you think it was your fault? Does patronizing others exonerate you from future pain?

I'll never ask. I will try to like you, if only for James sake for I may never know what exactly makes you tick, but tonight I am just too tired. Don't come over too early tomorrow, I think I would like to see you at the front door a little later in the day. I wonder if you would understand even if I told you how I feel?

It's scary to think maybe it wouldn't matter. Sometimes I wish we would be transferred to... well... maybe, Hawaii.

I put the last plate in the dishwasher, pressed the start button and the soothing hum of the wash cycle began. The stillness almost tasted good if that were possible. It was eleven o'clock at night and there was nothing needing my attention.

I climbed the stairs, went in the bedroom and plopped into bed, but in what seemed like no time morning came. Billy cried, Molly barked, the phone rang and the timer buzzed. When all was under control and the room was quiet, I stood and waited by the front door, but the doorbell too was silent.

In the Still of the Night

Maria grimaced as she squeezed her pregnant belly between the seat and the table. We worked at Kentucky Fried Chicken and were in charge of the restaurant for the day because the manager had taken the day off. The place was empty so we sat in a booth where we could keep our eyes on both entrances. It was after the lunch crowd left and before the afternoon early birds arrived so I grabbed a chicken leg, an extra crispy thigh, some coleslaw and mashed potatoes, and brought Maria a plate of the same.

Before she picked up the thigh she looked at me and asked me to tell her why my family had left Tennessee, a subject which, up to this time, I had avoided. Now having recently hinted about marriage I couldn't blame her for wanting to know. Reaching across the table I took her hands in mine. Rubbing my forefingers over her rough skin, toughened by years of picking grapes in the nearby fields, I felt very protective of her sitting there eating her coleslaw and smacking her lips like a swollen fish. Her shiny black hair framed her olive complexion and made her look near perfect. Pa would have said after downing a few belts, God damn near perfect. Sober, on one of his born again Christian days, with the worn Gideon Bible in hand, he'd more likely have said let us pray, with a lengthy explanation to God about the sins of man. Ma would undoubtedly have sat with her usual detached look of not being born the first time. But as Maria had never met anyone in my family, best I just begin at the beginning.

I gnawed on my chicken leg while Maria took another bite of her coleslaw and I proposed right then and there. I remember the words. I had heard them somewhere probably a movie.

Holding her hands in mine I said, "Will thou O Maria marry me?"

She didn't hesitate for a minute before she replied, "Ralphie Caldwell! I'd be ever so delighted."

I came around the table and kissed her full on the lips just like they do in the movies. She tasted like coleslaw.

It was early afternoon and still no customers, so I began to tell her the story right there as best I could recollect, thinking it might be wise to leave out some parts like Pa's yelling on his godless days and Ma's bossiness on all her days. I wiped my mouth, slicked back my hair, sat up straight and began.

We left the state of Tennessee in the middle of the night in the year 1963. But best I start the afternoon before, well maybe even a bit before that.

My family lived in Johnson County Tennessee until I was 12. The three-bedroom house was what we would call a shack here in California—the roof leaked, the floors were bare dirt, no hot water and an outhouse in back. We were always too hot in the summer and too cold in the winter, but things were like that back in Tennessee. We were poor. Pa picked fruit, mostly peaches, but even so the county helped us. Ma was blind so she couldn't do much. My sister did the chores and cooking.

Now it came to pass, (I got this sentence right out of the Gideon bible) that one day Ma called me from her chair by the window. I ran down the hall to see what she wanted, her voice penetrating my brain like an ice pick.

"Hold on Ma, I'm coming! I hear you." I wanted to say just shut up, for it was about the third time she had called me in half-an-hour, once just to find out where I was. This time she really needed me, for she had cut her finger on a piece of broken glass and it was bleeding all over her lap. I picked up a dingy rag from the floor and wrapped it around the finger and that seemed to do the trick. She sat back in her chair holding the bandage as she called for Sarah.

"Ma, she's in school. Pa's out back with old man Gentry picking apples. Should I get him?" The minute I mentioned Pa I knew that it was the wrong thing to say as she didn't answer, just slumped back in her chair, clutching her finger and turning her head toward the window. She could no longer see out of this window, nobody could it was too dirty, but Ma sat looking out just like she could. She would sit there for hours, her long sinewy dirt-streaked arms resting on the worn upholstered arms of the chair. She saw no need to ever clean her fingernails, wash her hair, or take a bath until it was necessary to relieve the itching. I used to think that she and the chair looked pretty much the same, like she was glued into it with remnants of sticky food. At one time she was probably a pretty woman but years of sitting had taken its toll. Yellow-grey strands highlighted her greasy brown hair. She had the look and smell of utter neglect, from her worn cotton dress right down to her threadbare slippers. Her life was simply somewhere else.

Following a loud knock on the door, Ma let out a noise like a screech owl, or maybe it just seemed like a screech owl. I'd never really heard one, only read about them, but anyway she sounded like something out of the animal kingdom—like she did every time anyone knocked at the door.

"Door Ralphie."

It was like she thought I couldn't hear. I opened the door just wide enough to see who it might be. A gust of cold air entered the house blowing the truant officer in with it.

"Ma, it's that man from school that ware here yesterday. Shall I ask him in?" But he was standing in front of her chair before she could answer. She raised her milky eyes, looking up as if she could really see him and said, "Well, what you all want today?"

Then she turned back to the window, her sign of dismissal, but the truant officer didn't leave.

"Mrs. Caldwell, it's Officer Shannon from the school. It's about Sally Jo, her teacher told me she hasn't been in school for two days. May I speak with her?" Ma kept looking out the window, just like she could see that hound dog humping the other one on the path outside, before she answered, "Ralphie, get baby sister."

"Okay," I answered and started walking toward the back of the house.

I had no idea where Sally Jo was. I hadn't seen her all day. I walked dutifully down the hallway banging a couple of doors like I was looking for her. I opened the back door to escape just in time for my Pa, still outside, to grab me by one arm and drag me back into the house.

"Ralphie, get the hell back in there your Ma needs you, turn yerself round." He pushed me toward the front room. I walked but Pa sort of stumbled behind for he had been drinking.

"Whast you-alls want?" He was holding himself upright in the doorway looking at the truant officer, but Ma didn't even turn her head. She just kept looking out the dirty window. I shifted my gaze to the floor and stood on one foot and then the other. The truant officer stood looking at Pa who was trying to focus his eyes.

"Mr. Caldwell, her teacher was concerned about Sally Jo, could we talk to her?"

"Shurch," Pa answered. But before Pa could say another word a terrible bang came from the back of the house. The room shook and the pictures on the walls trembled as they tilted. A moment later the diploma that Pa had bought for a dollar from the Santa Jane Society of Ministers, a holy document giving him full rights to preach the word of God, fell from its nail to the floor with a gentle thud.

I remembered when Pa framed this diploma and hung it on the wall and called himself a full-fledged minister of Everlasting Glory. He took to wearing suits and ties and even socks with his shoes on Sundays and holidays. He purchased this clothing at the second hand store, so nothing really fit but he dressed each Sunday as proper for a minister, from necktie to black shoes. He carried the word of God in a red Gideon bible ready to impress any heathen who might walk by him in Johnson County. There were some days when he drank a bit too much hooch and needed help just to walk. We all stayed out of his way during these days and this was one of them. His necktie was askew as he clutched the doorway. But, back to the big bang.

The truant officer's feet jumped clean up off the dirt floor, and when they landed he turned and ran like grease lightening right out the front door.

"I think it swere the shed." Pa said looking over his shoulder.

Well, I knew it were the shed but my mind was racing ahead wondering if Sally Jo had been in it. I pretended a calm I didn't feel, as I picked up the diploma, hung it back on the wall then casually stood up to the full height of my almost 12 years, fearful that the truant officer might have returned to announce to anyone who happened to be listening, "Oh this happens all the time. It's the, the stove, it sort of blows up when it overheats."

But Pa and the truant officer had gone their separate ways. I was about to leave when Ma finally turned around and squinted at me, "Ralphie . . . Ralphie—I'm hungry."

Just then the front door flew open and Sarah my older sister blew into the room, stamping her feet, her stringy yellow hair flying in every direction and her hands blue from the cold.

"Ma, it's me Sarah."

"Sarah, get my dinner. Ralphie, get your Pa in here."

It was a lucky move on the truant officers part that he had left when he did because a portion of the corrugated roof loosened by the bang suddenly gave way and fell to the floor directly over where he had been standing. Pa, reeled back into the house, watched and gave God a good piece of his mind as he looked up at the new vacancy in the roof and then walked back to look at the shed. Then returning from the rubble that had once been the shed, he turned and grabbed Ma by her shoulders.

"Ruby, get yer ass up off that there God-damn chair. Ralphie, start packing yer duds—we is getting out of this here place right now."

It was none too soon as the cold air coming in was penetrating our bones. Pa meant business, so we packed. I remember being so cold my hands hurt and Sarah's fair skin had turned an even darker blue.

That night we left Tennessee, all packed up in our old truck, just Sarah, Pa, Ma, and me. I was almost twelve, Sarah fifteen, and Sally Jo would have been ten had she been there—but unfortunately, I think she went up in smoke with the gin still.

I remember Pa's anger as he looked at our house and repeated, "Get your asses in gear all of you, we gotta be out of here by midnight."

And we were.

Ruby Caldwell had a window seat in the old truck so her complaints were at a minimum. I couldn't help but wonder how a change of scenery could interest a blind woman, but Ma just kept looking out as if engrossed in each changing scene. We worked picking fruit, slept in warm train stations or even abandoned barns as we made our way to California and reached there by early spring of 1963.

Pa turned to Ma when we crossed the border into California, like she could care where he pointed, he said, "Ruby take a look out there. We're in Cal-e-fer-ne-a. It didn't take us no time a tall. Now let's get to Fresno." But Ruby didn't answer.

My Pa had heard about Fresno, a warm agricultural area just right for farming, from Clem our neighbor in Johnson County who had a relative there. Within two days we drove into Fresno, our money almost completely gone, and the old truck not far behind.

*   *   *

In Fresno Pa and I stood in line at the welfare department and upon reaching the receptionist at the front desk, she said, "Please Mr. Caldwell just step this way. You may bring your boy with you."

"It's Reverend, Church of Eternal Grace," he corrected her.

"Oh, I beg your pardon Reverend—if you'll just step this way and fill out these papers and I will call a Social Worker."

But before she could leave, the Reverend spoke up, "Miss there, I, uh, I may be in need of some help. I don't read so good."

Pa could read only a tad better than he could write and he couldn't write at all, which the social worker picked up on immediately. I sat in the corner while she filled out the papers with his answers, and when they were finished we walked back to the truck. Ma and Sarah looked exhausted, and I was pretty tired myself.

Within two weeks my family had a little house with the help of subsidized housing, government food stamps to help with groceries, and my Pa got a part-time job picking grapes. Sarah and I were in school. We were all on public assistance and our social worker, Mrs. Robinson, visited us weekly with help and suggestions. Ma sat on a new chair, looking out a clean glass window overlooking a beautiful vineyard. The worker brought her a new cotton dress, well—new to her, and leather slippers, which she accepted without even a thank you. I don't think Ma knew much about getting gifts. The social worker just seemed pleased that they fit. I was happy to see her in a new chair that didn't smell.

I often hid behind a door in the kitchen and listened while Mrs. Robinson and Ma talked. It wasn't an easy job talking to Ma as she didn't do much talking and even less answering. But I guess she liked the worker—a young woman with a pleasant way about her. Gradually I learned lots of new things about Pa and Ma, like when they lived in Tennessee they had given their first child away when Ma was only 13 because they had no money to feed him. How Pa had been in trouble with the law when a little girl complained about him touching her and how Ma hated sex! This last bit of knowledge I could have done without, but if you are an eavesdropper you take what you gets.

Mrs. Robinson talked to Ma about Pa and things I knew I shouldn't be hearing, but that never stopped me from listening. One day when Pa was away, Ma said to Mrs. Robinson, "Jim Caldwell is a mean man and I'm afeared of him." Then fearing she had said too much she hung her head and refused to speak any more. Mrs. Robinson left, but not before she gave Ma an understanding pat on her shoulder.

If I remember rightly I think it was around this time that ten year-old Melody who lived down the street came up missing. I learned later she had complained to her parents of the Reverent Caldwell putting his hands inside her panties when he told her about God. Her parents contacted the police who questioned the neighbors and learned that The Reverend has been seen on the street talking to Melody the day before she disappeared. Melody's father contacted Mrs. Robinson who contacted the Johnson County police and verified that there had been child molesting accusations against Pa back in Johnson County, so the Fresno police took it from there.

It was after school and I was behind the kitchen door once more listening to two policemen. I couldn't quite hear all they said but I had no trouble hearing Pa's replies.

"Yes I remember her. She was rude to me and I had to hit her, that's all God says—you spare the rod you spoil the child. No, I didn't hurt her. No, I ain't seen her since."

It was a week later that Melody's body was found in a nearby vacant lot where Pa said he had last seen her. He admitted hitting her, perhaps a bit too hard but claimed no way did he kill her. He had to go to court. When questioned in court Pa declared he had nothing to do with her death and he tried to convince the court psychiatrist her death was a punishment from God. I think this was his free ticket to Atascadero prison for rehabilitation.

I overheard the policemen say that a semen sample on the girl's body proved to be Pa's. The policemen said that during the whole drive to Atascadero my Pa proclaimed his innocence and had a lengthy one-sided conversation with the devil after which he walked proudly into the prison carrying his old worn Gideon Bible. I heard all of this in bits and pieces from my usual hiding place behind the kitchen door, after the two policemen stepped into the kitchen out of earshot of Ma.

My sister and I finished high school in Fresno. Sarah shopped and cooked for us and cared for our Ma, and I helped as much as I could. Mrs. Robinson arranged for a county caretaker to care for Ma while we were in school, and when Sarah left for Tennessee to marry her childhood sweetheart, my mother went to a home for the blind. I see her now about once a month, but I have seen Pa only once in the past five years.

I took him a box of candy that first Christmas. It was a nice prison where Pa went to rehabilitate. He insisted he didn't know why. Sarah refused to visit him, and I was afraid to ever ask her why.

Back at the KFC, Maria reached over and took my hand in hers. "Oh Ralphie, my old man has been in jail too, for stealing cars and I think for beating my mother, but he ran away when he got out and we've never seen him since. My mother won't talk about him." She looked into my eyes with understanding and tried to be of comfort and as I finished the story she held my hand tightly in hers.

I felt comfortable with Maria as I continued, "I graduated from high school and by now you pretty well know the rest. Ma is living in the home for the blind and sitting by another window. She has a thing for windows. She never asks about Pa or us kids, or what is outside. Maybe she sees whatever she wants, or again maybe she doesn't see anything, the doctor in the home did say she is totally blind. In a way, isn't this true for many of us? Pa died in prison last year, and although his eyesight was perfect he never saw and probably never believed what he had done. When I told Ma that Pa had passed, she just shrugged her shoulders and went right on looking out to her world outside."

*   *   *

After we were married, Maria asked to visit her mother-in-law. The next day we went to the home.

I told Ma who Maria was and that we had a baby. Ma turned toward us for just a moment absently tapping her knee with one hand before she turned back to look out the window. She never moved her head or made even a gesture to look at her grandchild. She didn't even speak to either Maria or me, but just kept tapping her knee. It was like we weren't there. Maybe she was homesick for Tennessee.

My Friend

Backward turn backward,
Oh time in thy flight,
Make me a child again,
Just for tonight.

—Elizabeth Akers Allen

Dear Jane,

Just for fun I decided to turn back the clock and look at us over my shoulder. In our day, nobody wrote much about puberty, but if I remember rightly we laughed ourselves right through our teen years. I was twelve before I realized I had a body. I was nearly thirteen when my family moved to a new town in California. There I entered a new school, where I met you. That was around sixty-five years ago.

Everything changed for me almost at once. My body began to grow soft hair under my arms and in the pubic region. My breasts, however, were my greatest concern. One breast started to grow before the other, causing me great consternation. I worried that I would have to enter a new school with no friends and a lopsided chest. I couldn't tell my mother, I simply didn't discuss those things with her, and besides I didn't want her to know I was a freak. It was a relief when within a very few weeks, breast number two popped forth and caught up to the other one. I never told anyone. Well, maybe I did tell you, Jane. It was around that same time that mother gave me the book called *Growing Up*, which acquainted me with the rest of the transformation information and reached me just in the nick of time. Midst all this, my family had settled in South Pasadena with me tagging along, biological changes and all.

The best thing that happened after the move was that I met you, my very best friend, and we would form a friendship that would last all of our lives. It was 1942, America's second year into World War Two. The public school where we met was in an upper class suburban area of Los Angeles County. The building was a large cement edifice, the hallways lined with lockers. The schoolroom doors had black numbers painted at eyelevel. There was an odor, not entirely unpleasant of shoes, coats and books permeating the hallways.

As my surname began with F and yours with G we were seated next to each other in homeroom and our friendship developed quickly, nourished by the fact we were both new to the school and found ourselves floundering among students who had been together since the first grade. Getting asked into that elite social strata would be like an invitation to court from Queen Elizabeth today. But, be that as it may, you and I found that we had opted for nearly the same classes and really didn't miss the fraternization with, "from the first grade together rah-rah club."

*   *   *

It is always easier to look back and too hard, if not virtually impossible, to look forward with any certainty. But I digress. Whichever way you look at it, school in this country is not the same today for the teenager as it was over half a century ago. Back in those days we were not known as teenagers, our years were designated only numerically. Puberty was an unused word outside our vocabulary. Girls wore dresses, never slacks or jeans. Classes were purely academic, with the exception of typing and shorthand. Sex education was limited to a few sentences in biology and that consisted of telling us there were two of them. Just an interesting vignette; only one high school girl got pregnant and she was an import from somewhere out of state. Nobody thought to befriend her. You and I were most amazed that she had done it but never thought to approach her. The whole school gave her a wide berth if you will excuse the pun on so serious a catastrophe.

I'll try to tell you how I remember us and you can form your own picture. We wore knee-length cotton skirts with white blouses in the spring and pleated wool skirts and warm sweaters in the winter, and always saddle shoes and white bobby sox. The picture is completed when you count a couple of notebooks and probably a small purse lodged in our arms. You were far daintier than I with your hourglass figure, brown hair and eyes a beautiful shade of brown. I had blue eyes an overabundance of curly Irish brown hair and was just thankful my body was no longer asymmetrical. Fortunately both of us had clear skin, not like the poor girl who sat across from me in homeroom with pimples like headlights. Her name was Edith. She really needed some Noxema medicated cream to cover those lights and could easily have bought some at H. S. Kress store for less than a dollar. I wanted so to tell her but knew enough to let that one go. Her mind was as brilliant as the pimples, and she later became class valedictorian. It's funny how you remember those things after all this time.

You and I were about the same height, but I was more on the athletic side, which is simply my way of saying I was bigger. Even my shoes were bigger. Our ability to laugh at almost anything we said or did made life a roller coaster, and we would often walk down the street after school literally bent over double in spasms of giggles stemming from an unknown etiologies even to ourselves.

In our last year of high school you had a boyfriend named Sterling. I remember we referred to him as Sterling Silver. And I had somebody named Damon. His last name was Lilly so we changed his first name to Silly. And then occasionally we would have a blind date with a boy from the Navy. These blind dates were acquired through our friend Betty who was engaged to a sailor named Dick. Don't forget it was wartime and sailors were plentiful. The local high school boys looked terribly mundane beside the knights and gladiators furnished by the enlisted men of U. S. Navy.

But back to high school. We had two other close friends, Dorothy and Betty. We often went to Balboa beach together on a Saturday where we baked to a flaming red and then admired out suntans. But you and I were the closest. I was an only child. I don't remember seeing your older brother much. I used to think we were as close as sisters, but now that I have four girls of my own I think maybe we were closer as there was never any competition between us. Perhaps this stems from not having the same mother.

Our high school campus was bereft of graffiti, alcohol, mind-altering drugs or lethal weapons. The absence of any sex education classes eliminated any creative homework in that course. Of course there will always be extracurricular volunteer activities found in any discipline wherever you are in time or space. But in the 1940s our fun was harmless to ourselves, or to others, and most of all we had time to create and dream dreams. School dances were chaperoned due to decorum, not to possible police entanglement with peer group lawbreakers.

I don't think we knew the word condom, although I am sure the sailors in town did, but the ones we met respected or probably feared our parents and most probably were as green as we were.

I think my favorite class was English. You might have liked French better, but I don't know. Our English teacher was Miss Hayslip, who wore an auburn wig always slightly askew and whose wardrobe consisted, at the most, of two dresses. She was not a great dresser but a great teacher. We sat in old-fashioned desks attached to each other front to back on runners like railroad tracks. Well anyway, you and I sat in the row by the windows with papers all over our desks and one warm day when the windows were open the idea occurred to one of us to throw our papers out the windows one at a time whenever Miss Hayslip turned her back. This was such great fun that within the hour when class was finished our complete notebooks, page by page, were two stories down on a cement walkway. We spend the next period picking them all up. We thought we were funnier than the Marx Brothers.

Laughing until we hurt was our specialty. We even laughed through our graduation ceremony, quivering under caps and gowns. When you turned to me just before we paraded on stage for this serious rite of passage, you said, "No squat, no squint, no stoop." (The logo for Philco radio.) We stifled our laughter every time we looked at each other throughout the entire ceremony. High school had been comparatively worry-free for two giggling growing girls.

We often spent our Saturdays at the beach or bicycling through the park or at the movies, or if it rained at one of our homes, playing card games. You had an archery set and there was a tennis court in a park near my house. We played popular 78 records on a turntable record player, the kind with a changeable needle secured into an arm that bent back and forward in order to place the needle directly on the grooves of a revolving record. I remember you singing Elmer's Tune and how we wallowed in these sad wartime love songs, emitting deep emotional sighs over the world's greatest emotion, love.

Sometimes we hung out after school at Fosselman's, the local ice cream parlor. We had plenty of leisure time. I don't remember ever being exhausted from being rushed from one extracurricular activity to another, corralled by parental pressure, to overachieve in competitive peer activities. When I think of the free time we had, because of the structured competitive and compulsory activities that were not required of us, well, it may explain why life is so stressful for the children today.

To our credit we both went on to Ivy League Colleges, for despite all this laughter, we had made good grades, and midst all this laughter, a natural growth took place at a pace that would prepare us emotionally for the days of higher education, followed by marriage and parenthood.

What a difference between the schools of yesterday and those of today. Is it possible that society today demands too much insignificant pressure on our youth, heaping their plates too high with academia, and this coupled with too many activities leaves too little time for self-creative play and relaxation? Perhaps it is time to throw some of our papers out the window once more.

Maybe not all but just some, but then what do we choose? It's a moot question.

Jane, we have always found something to laugh about and that's what counts. I am glad we went to school together and sat by that open window in the time and place when we did.

Love you for being my best friend,
Patty

Not Guilty

Preface

It was Saturday mid-morning when she got into her Jaguar, turned on the radio and headed toward St Francis Woods. About half way across the Golden Gate Bridge a news report jolted Margaret back eleven years to a time she hardly ever thought of, except maybe when she heard a grandfather clock strike. The announcer was reporting an attack in San Francisco by a pit bull on an eleven year-old girl. The child was in critical condition after being mauled and badly bitten. A young boy had been bitten when he tried to pull the dog off the girl. She reached over and turned up the volume after the announcer named the child's parents, Harold and Julia Halley. She tried to convince herself that it was probably just a coincidence but doubted it. Halley was hardly a popular name, not like Smith or Jones, anyway. It could be another Halley family but the child was the right age and right name. When the weather forecast came on she turned off the radio. It seemed like forever before she drove into the driveway of her old home and picked up her mother.

1

Margaret and her husband lived in Marin County, just outside San Francisco, California, in the town of Tiberon, known for its art nouveau, avant-garde artists and eschewal of cheap, tasteless, or in any way common people or their lifestyles. With the exception of art nouveau, Margaret identified with the town. Her home was professionally decorated with contemporary furniture and Italian artwork. A beautiful ocean view of San Francisco and the bay can be seen from the front balcony.

Her mother, Janice Lowell was forty-two when she became pregnant with Margaret, a complete surprise to a couple who had given up ever having children and, as is often the case, the child was overindulged and by age three, pretty much the princess of the castle. To say she was a snob, either as a young girl or an adult, would be wrong, for she simply expected and got the best without giving thought to the alternative. Perhaps a better word was spoiled, having been given too much and denied so little. Margaret sailed smoothly through school, finishing with a degree in Art History from Mills College, a private girls' school across the bay. It was important for her to dress well, give elegant parties, and decorate her home with the finest of furnishings. Facials and manicures kept her groomed to perfection, while massages, tennis, golf and horseback riding kept her figure svelte. She would never allow herself to be called Maggie.

The song *Five Feet Two Eyes of Blue* could have been written for her. She was thin but shapely, with features just a tad this side of beautiful—dark hair, blue eyes, a turned up nose and a smile revealing small, straight white teeth. She looked younger than her thirty-three years. Her ancestors originated in the British Isles as evidenced by portraits of Dukes, Earls, and aristocratic landholders ascending the wall beside the staircase to the second floor of the house in St. Francis Woods where she grew up.

Her husband Sidney was a highly successful attorney. His piercing blue eyes could hold a jury captive throughout the longest of summations. Sidney was the type of man who appeared taller than he was and presented himself in the military manner of an officer and a gentleman. He was considered one of the finest trial lawyers in the area, known for his silver tongued arguments and a high batting average of successes. He too, had been raised in opulence as his family, German in origin, had made a fortune in the South African diamond mines before moving to America. The family settled in Palo Alto, California, and both he and his father were Stanford University graduates.

As she stood on her balcony and looked out over the bay toward San Francisco, she thought back to the dinner party when she met Sidney's parents. It was her dad's birthday and her mother had invited another couple, Helmet and Helene Crowl, to join them at a surprise dinner for her husband in this posh restaurant with its magnificent view of The City and the bay. When Margaret and her parents were seated and waiting for the guests, Margaret looked around the room and out the window at the sparkling lights of San Francisco nineteen stories below. The low hum of voices in the busy restaurant and the view outside made it seem like a different world. Her dress with gold trimming was brand new and she ventured a peek under the table to admire her new gold high heel shoes, before she turned to her father to mouth a soft, "Happy birthday Dad." Behind her father a couple was approaching their table from across the room. Maurice felt the man tap him on his shoulder and he stood up in amazement when he recognized his friends.

"If it isn't Helmut and Helene Crowl, what are you doing here? This is really a surprise, I haven't seen you for ages, old man."

The men shook hands and Helene greeted Janice with a knowing smile and a wink before she turned to her husband. "Well, Janice said it was your birthday, so we thought we'd help you celebrate. You're never too old for a birthday, Maurice old man."

Helene was a tall grey-haired woman with a nose too large for her face, but friendly brown eyes softened the bird-like appearance it gave her. Helmut on the other hand came across like a rotund German waiter, and when he laughed, you could picture him at the Oktoberfest in Munich—a white apron around his waist, holding a stein of foaming beer in each hand—a somewhat incongruent description, with the exception of the apron, of a man in his profession—a dentist.

A solicitous waiter brought two more chairs and Helmut and Helene joined the table. Margaret would soon learn that her father had gone to college with Helmut.

"Helmet old boy, I must tell you that we just returned from three months in Europe. Saw Heidelberg and it hasn't changed much, but I guess old castles never do."

Helmet turned to Margaret.

"Did you enjoy Germany?"

"Oh, I didn't go..."

But before I could say anymore, Janice interrupted, "She graduated from college and stayed home to get some well-deserved rest. We are terribly proud of her; she did so well in school."

The dinner conversation was devoted to heartfelt laughter of the good old days of yesteryear, with memories bringing back even more memories. On the way down on the elevator Janice turned to Helene and enquired about her son.

"How's Sidney?"

"Oh Janice, he's just fine—let's get together for lunch. I want to hear all about your daughter too, it's been too long. I'll call you."

The following week during their luncheon date, Janice and Helene decided to introduce their children to each other.

Four years later Sidney and Margaret were married, preceded by a barrage of engagement parties, tea parties and showers, and at last, when the festivities were over it was a relief to both families—although neither admitted it. Unbeknownst to the bride and groom, it would prove to be a fortuitous match of fate for one young girl.

2

It was raining outside when Sidney came home from his office in San Francisco, and told his wife that the parents of a child who had been mauled by a pit bull had been in to see him. He went on to say he had seen them that morning.

"The child is recovering although she will be scarred for life. The police were unable to find a trace of the dog or its owners. There is a leash law in San Francisco. The parents tell me the owners were not in sight and the dog was running loose. The child Nancy was, a very pretty little girl. Her mother showed me pictures of her before and after. It was pretty awful." He grimaced before he continued, "The family only moved here a couple of years ago from Colorado. It is a real tragedy." He had not been looking at Margaret, or he would have seen the stricken look on his wife's face.

She heard very little after learning the child's name but as Sidney's eyes were busy perusing the paper he failed to notice her face had turned ashen and her hands trembled ever so slightly.

He shook his head, folded the paper and put it on the seat beside him before looking up to continue, "Why people have pit bulls is beyond me. And why they let children play with them is way beyond me. Not that these parents let her play with it. According to the mother it happened so fast she didn't know it until the dog ran out from behind the house and had her child down on the sidewalk."

Margaret just looked at him and he read her face as sympathetic concern.

"How awful, Sidney—are you going to take the case?" Stretching his legs out in front and his arms over his head he took a deep breath before righting himself back to a sitting position.

"I told them I would."

All she could think of to say was, "Was there a police report?"

"The police report was fairly short and disclosed only that the Halley's lived in a residential area in San Francisco. Mr. Halley said the dog lived next door, but the house had been vacated. The report stated that the owners had left no forwarding address. Mrs. Halley stated that she had seen the dog over a side fence just the day before and was surprised to see it out on the street. An eight year-old boy, James Uldridge, tried to pull it off of the girl, but was bitten in the attempt. Both children were taken to the hospital where the boy, with only minor injuries, was released to his father."

Words failed her so she shook her head and found herself asking Sidney if he would like a Martini, but before he could answer she found herself making one for each of them.

The conversation turned to other things, but Mrs. Crowl paid little attention. Sidney could have told her the British were coming and she might have just nodded. He did pick up on the fact that something was wrong, but based it on the fact that her parents were coming to dinner the next day, he knew this always worried her. When he questioned her, she told him she was thinking about what to serve, as her mother was always so critical of her cooking.

Sidney was older than Margaret, fifteen years to be exact, and had a grown son James from a previous marriage who was now a medical student in Boston. He had divorced James's mother when their child was five. The first Mrs. Sidney Crowl lived in New York, aspiring to be an actress, addicted to drugs and alcohol for at least seventeen years and through two more unsuccessful marriages. She was so debilitated, she couldn't make it to her son's graduation from college, but nobody seemed to care much.

Somehow Margaret had never been able to speak of either her marriage or Nancy to anyone. Why couldn't she? Why didn't she? She simply did not know. Perhaps she hoped maybe that part of her life would just dissolve if she never shared it, but it hadn't.

Sidney had been married before so he would understand, but Margaret's rational of never mentioning her marriage was simply that you can't talk about something that never was, and hers had been annulled so it really never was. If somehow it ever were to come up, but it probably wouldn't, she planned to say Dan was a research chemist. Well, he did mix substances. What a wonderful thing the spoken word is to convey incorrect information to others, almost on a par with the unspoken unreasonable rational thoughts to oneself.

That night she tossed and turned, would morning ever come? It finally did and after Sidney left for work she straightened up the house, but her heart wasn't in it.

3

After the fog had lifted on the bay outside Tiberon, Margaret stood alone on her terrace looking over the balustrade at the expanse of water. Her mind went back twelve years to St.

Francis Woods. She had just finished college and had come back home to live.

It was in the time that would always be referred to as the hippie era, the 1960s. It was summer and her parents traveled abroad on an extended trip through Europe. When they returned three months later, she announced she was thinking of marrying Dan Stalwell. Her father brightened up immediately.

"Stalwell of Stalwell and Son?"

She hesitated but answered truthfully, "Well, no Dad, Dan is a bartender."

At this her mother did all but faint and her father stood up and looked her straight in the face, "Why haven't I met this young man?"

She remembered stepping backward as his nose came closer to her face. "Daddy, you have been in Europe for the last three months, you weren't even here!"

That evening after a vociferous confrontation with both parents she ran upstairs and phoned Dan, and when she heard his car drive up, she stole out of the house, jumped in beside him and they left for Reno. The rain was torrential—thunder cracked and lightning sent unruly flashes of blue and yellow across the sky, but nothing seemed as frightening as the altercation she had just left. Her father had threatened to disown her. Her mother had wrung her hands in anguish. She had tried to explain that she needed to be free to do her own thing, to no longer follow conventions but her parents were just too conventional to even listen.

After getting married in Reno, they drove right to Colorado where Dan plied his trade as a bartender and they lived in a rented mobile home.

Her marriage had been rocky from the beginning, but Margaret was not about to admit to herself, or worse yet to her parents, that she had made a mistake, or possible two mistakes. Had she thought about it she might have blamed her second mistake—the marriage—on the storm. Thunder had always unnerved her. If it had not been for that and the torrential rain she would certainly have known - but the marriage was not all of her problem.

She met Dan at a bar when she and some girl friends had gone to the Haight-Ashbury district in San Francisco. After a few drinks she found herself waking up in a lumpy bed with the sun streaming through a dingy window into an even dingier room, and standing over her was, of all people, Dan the bartender. He didn't look at all dingy, in fact standing there in his underwear he looked like a Greek God to her. She blinked her eyes. Her drinks had been numerous but not enough to cause the horrific headache she was feeling. She had a hunch she had been drugged, which made the seduction a little easier to swallow, as it was not really her fault. Her parents were in Europe, which made it easy to see Dan frequently during the next three months. She was in love. She marveled at the tattoo of a jungle cat on his left arm, a cat with its claws extended. A cat she named Her Danny Boy.

Margaret had driven him by the house where she lived but never invited him inside. He was her secret even from the house and something she owned all by herself. Daddy wouldn't admonish her for his poor grammar, and Mother wouldn't judge him by his long hair or lack of upper class genealogy. Neither one would have the opportunity to give a lengthy diatribe on the tattoo, his parents, education, religion or dress code. Why? Because she vowed they would never meet him.

When he asked her to marry him she said yes right away. Just imagine the life of passion that would ensue. It was also the answer to a problem that been consuming her, a problem that was making her sick, really sick in the mornings.

That summer, with her parents out of the country, she had felt as free as a bird as she perused the streets of the Haight-Ashbury—that little magical area of San Francisco labeling its inhabitants the flower children; youth soliciting escape from the yokes and mores of society by exalting in the drug culture and complete freedom of speech, dress, and sex.

These flowers walked the streets day and night, many with the help of chemical substances. Some talking to themselves, others weaving about in weird medieval costumes convincing themselves and anybody who could listen how happy they were to be free of any links to their constraining habitats or socioeconomic status. They overlooked the fact that flowers come from plants rooted in the earth—they just don't float around the air on psychedelic drugs and survive. She only smoked marijuana, had tried LSD once with an unfavorable result, and then never used anything stronger. Dan liked the weed but claimed not to really use anything else. Perhaps.

The marriage lasted six months, and when Margaret and the baby came back to their mobile home from the hospital in Lone Tree Colorado, Dan and his belongings were nowhere to be found. There was a five-dollar bill on the shabby dresser. The baby was a girl, and Margaret looked at her with disdain. Of course it was not the baby's fault, but Margaret was not used to accepting the blame for much of anything, and the only other person in the room at the time was the baby. Looking the eight-pound bundle right in the face she spoke, "How could you do this to me?" The baby's only answer was a lusty cry.

The next day she walked to a neighbor, borrowed her phone and placed a collect call to her father explaining she had left Dan and wanted to come home. His retort was far gentler with more warmth then she had expected.

"We have been worried sick about you, glad you've left that Dan whatever his name is. Got wise to him, eh? Good!! Now get the hell home where you belong."

Her father didn't sound too angry, and she was glad now that she had sent her parents those few postcards with innocuous little tidbits from Colorado—but never a word about her pregnancy. She found Dan working that night at the bar and he was agreeable with her plan so her next call was to an adoption agency.

The name of the baby on the birth certificate was Nancy. When she and Dan left from the Judge's chambers, Nancy's parents were no longer Daniel and Margaret Stalwell but Julia and Harold Halley. Dan left immediately after the papers were signed and she never saw him again.

Across the little town of Lone Tree a grandfather clock in the hallway was chiming twelve o'clock noon, a dirge-like bonging that went on and on reverberating in her head until she was clear of the Halley's house and in her car. Mrs. Halley had insisted that she see what a nice room Nancy would have, and invited her to follow her across the hall to a pink and white nursery. Having seen the child's room, she took her leave just as the grandfather clock in the hallway finished chiming. For only a brief moment she had harbored a little uncertainty, but knowing her parents it would be far better to return home empty-handed. Eventually she came to believe that she hadn't kept the baby because of her parents, thus, once again, exonerating herself from guilt. The real truth was she simply didn't want a baby.

Not only did she not tell her parents about the baby, she didn't share that Dan had been the one to walk out on her. She knew her father would have done a lot of throat clearing and deep-throated hums before he decided to sue the shit out of that bastard bartender, and she wanted to save Daddy from all this worry. Besides it didn't look good for her image if Dan had left her.

Still standing on the balcony grasping the iron railing, she remembered how her parents had met her with open arms when she had returned to San Francisco. The first thing her mother said in the car after meeting her at the airport was, "I think you've put on a little weight."

"Okay Mom, I'll take it off."

They spoke very little on the way home. When Margaret climbed the staircase up to her old room, passing all the ancestors looking out benignly from inside their elegant gold frames, she kicked off her shoes and threw herself down on the bed. In a few minutes she stood up and examined her figure in the full-length mirror, and decided her mother was actually right.

The next day she found her old tennis racket and went to the country club to hit a few balls against the backboard. A woman with a baby in a stroller watched from behind the fence. When Margaret saw the baby she felt a little tug under her ribs, sort of an empty feeling around where her heart should have been, so when the ball gently bounced back she gave it a mighty wallop, sending it crashing against the backboard. She hadn't given a thought to Dan, but Nancy was a little harder to swat out of her life. The ball, returning from the backboard, rolled swiftly by her feet before it came to a stop in the grass just out of reach.

Soon she was legally free and clear of Dan after obtaining an annulment with the help of an attorney friend of her fathers. It was like Dan had never been. It was like the squalid little mobile home had never been. She convinced herself that she had never loved Dan anyway and soon felt like her old self. Without a doubt she now knew it had been the right decision to return home. She left the balcony and went shopping.

4

Three weeks after the pit bull attack, the mailman arrived with a registered letter for her. She opened it to a typewritten note. After reading it twice she crumpled it up and put it in her purse.

Dear Mrs. Crowl,
I need to see you regarding Nancy. Please meet me Wednesday at noon at Spenger's on 4th Street in Berkeley.
Thank you,
Julia Halley

How did Mrs. Halley know where to reach her and what for? Then it dawned on her. Of course! It was her picture on Sidney's desk. Mrs. Halley had recognized the picture of Nancy's birth mother—but what did she want with her? Had she mentioned anything to Sidney? Probably not—it would have been awkward to say, "Oh by the way Mr. Crowl, I have your wife's baby."

She was apprehensive about meeting Mrs. Halley again—and even more about telling Sidney—but told herself she would just go to see what she wanted and then maybe then tell Sidney the story.

It had been six years since Maurice's birthday dinner at the St. Francis and Mr. and Mrs. Sidney Crowl had been married almost two years. Should she now tell Sidney about Nancy? It almost seemed too late. Sitting on the balcony, her favorite refuge, with her elbows on the table and her chin resting in her hands she looked out over the balcony to the ocean, deep in thought. The bangles on her arms clinked together in agreement as she silently mouthed, "No, no need." She wondered if she might feel differently after seeing Julia Halley, but after debating with herself she decided to meet Mrs. Halley at the fish grotto.

She waited inside Spenger's in Berkeley for forty-five minutes, and when Julia failed to appear she left. But someone had been watching her from a parked car two isles away and when she got back into her Porsche and left, a Ford station wagon followed her.

The next two weeks went by without incident. With a couple of lunches at the country club, a facial and a manicure, she was beginning to feel like her old self. Sidney was working hard and often came home late, but he spoke little about his work usually just plopping himself down in a chair and opening the Chronicle.

When Margaret asked him about the Pitt Bull case, he said he had never handled a case for so many nonexistent people. Even the dog was nowhere to be found. The newspaper had dropped the story with the words that both dog and its owners were nowhere to be found. Margaret told herself that Nancy was probably fine, and that was all Julia Halley had wanted to tell her at Spenger's. So with this thought in mind she planned to enjoy—as she put it to herself—the rest of her life with Sidney. They would go to Paris, the French Riviera, and the South Pacific. She smiled as she cooked dinner that night. He smiled as they made love after dinner.

5

It was dusk and she sat at her husband's desk in the living room. Two weeks had passed since Sidney died. Time rolled back to the evening the night janitor found him. She had just finished making ravioli for dinner when the phone rang. The voice on the other end identified himself as a policeman with news that Sidney had been rushed to St. Francis Hospital in San Francisco with a gunshot wound to the chest, and she should get there as soon as possible.

In a state of shock she phoned her mother, cancelled their dinner explaining that Sidney was in the hospital, and she would get right back to her. After a quick goodbye she rushed out the front door.

At the hospital she attended to the necessary procedures at the front desk, then found herself standing outside the emergency room door looking through the glass at her husband on a gurney, the sole attention of a cluster of doctors. It seemed everything moving was in green. Sometime later one of the green-smocked doctors came out in the hall, put his hand on her shoulder and said, "I am terribly sorry Mrs. Crowl, we did all we could." Her extremities turned to gelatin.

Then, before reality set in, a policeman approached her and suggested they sit in the lobby. As he questioned her, he seemed oblivious to her feelings and it occurred to her that she might be a suspect. Maybe his calloused manner was just a ploy, like in detective stories, a ploy used by the police to elicit a confession. This policeman was very young and when Margaret looked at him closely she realized that he was just trying to do his job. She also found herself crying.

"No, I can't imagine who would want to kill him. No he doesn't—excuse me, didn't—tell me about his cases . . . well except what was already in the paper about the little girl and the dog." The policeman looked at her quizzically, so she said something about it being in the Chronicle a few weeks ago. Then fishing in her purse for a Kleenex she started to cry again.

By now it was nearly midnight. The policeman drove her home as she was shaking too badly to drive. The hard thing had been walking in the front door of the empty house. The light was blinking on the answering machine. The policemen stood with her as she pressed the message button and heard the time announced. It was five-o'clock in the evening—four hours ago— the voice was Sidney's.

"I'll be a little late, just leaving the office. Tell Mom and Dad I'll be there ASAP."

As Sidney's voice was coming out of that little black box in Tiberon, Margaret looked at the telephone and saw her husband in little pieces—his voice here, his body elsewhere, his soul probably yet another place. Her mind formed a scenario of how it must feel to be crazy. Little pieces of your whole being just going around in circles—never stopping, just swooping about in a voice.

In the days that followed Margaret managed to make the necessary arrangements from the obituary to the funeral to the burial. Now back home after the funeral, she threw her coat on the couch and looked at herself in the mirror. Black was very becoming. But today she hated it.

In a short time the Crowl family, as well as her parents, arrived with a number of Sidney's friends and colleagues. A buffet table was set with the proper repast for post-funeral gatherings. She was very tired, and when everyone left she was relieved to be alone. Her heart went out to Sidney's son, a young man who was very solicitous toward her, and she wished she had gotten to know him sooner. This led to thoughts of Nancy and she wondered if she should have told Sidney about her. Now she had no choice and it was not a comfort.

Her mother looked at her after the mourners had left and exclaimed, "Have you lost weight? You are too thin. You need a new black dress."

Margaret looked at her before replying, thinking how she wished she had a mother with empathy, one she could have told about the baby she had given away, as well as the husband who had left her. However, somewhere deep inside she didn't want to talk about any of it, and last but not least about the dog mauling. Nancy, and Sidney being the lawyer for her real "grandchild?" Instinctively she knew her mother was not the one with whom to share this information. Best let her think she was anorexic or bulimic or whatever.

"Yes mother, I think so."

"I think you had right better come home and live with your father and me."

6

A little girl of eleven was sitting up in bed in a hospital. Her bandages had been removed from the lacerations on her face and arms, although her head was still swathed, mostly because one ear had been torn off and there were deep puncture bites in her scalp. Nancy tried to smile when her mother came in the room, but despite her efforts only one side of her mouth cooperated.

It had been what seemed like many days since the dog had attacked her. Nancy looked at her mother and her torn lips caused the words to come out slurred. "Where ish Daddy, ish he home yet?"

"Any day now I know he wants to see you." Julia knew she was lying to her, but could she tell her daughter that her father could not stand the sight of her and had fled the scene? Certainly not—no, never. She loved this little girl and she must never know that her father found it abhorrent to look at her. She smiled lovingly at the pathetic bundle of bandaged child and handed her a box.

"Look Nancy, a new nightgown." Nancy fingered he soft cotton gown.

"Thanks, Mom. When can I come home? Where ish the neighbors' dog?"

Julia answered truthfully, "I don't know."

Nancy's hand went to her face and moved along the bandages on the right side of her head, stopping at the place where her ear used to be. "Mama will the dog be killed?"

"I don't think so. Here try on your nightgown."

"Maybe he will go to rehab like Daddy. Do they have rehab for dogs?"

Julia thought they should have gas chambers, but replied, "Dogs don't have rehab, guess they wouldn't understand.

"But daddy went to rehab."

Sure thought Julia—and he didn't get it either—but said instead, "He had to leave on a trip to Mexico. Nancy honey, is there anything I can bring you? Your class sent you a card. I was so anxious to see you that I forgot to put it in my purse. I'll bring it tomorrow." She stayed until Nancy finished her lunch, then said goodbye at the door. The doctor stopped her in the waiting room.

"Mrs. Halley may I speak to you for a moment?"

Julia was dumbstruck when she learned Nancy would need a kidney transplant, and as soon as possible. She immediately went to the lab to be tested to see if she could be a donor, then drove home. She left her car in the driveway and walked to the front of the house.

Stepping over the fading bloodstains on the sidewalk and quickly diverting her eyes to the sky, she thought, "Why Nancy?" A useless question followed by another one even more useless, "Where is Harold when I need support?" She had not heard from him since they had admitted Nancy to the hospital. She knew the answer as if God had spoken from the heavens, "He is drunk."

From a cave to the castle, whatever has housed one's family can be such a lonely place when it's empty. The walls reverberate with memories. Silence conjures up visions of those who lived there. Now Julia needed to think and she did this best with the aid of a deck of playing cards. Things often came to her while playing solitaire. She sat at the table and shuffled the cards as she wondered just how many people knew that each king in the deck represented a great king from history; Spades—King David; Clubs—Alexander the Great; Hearts—Charlemagne; Diamonds—Julius Caesar.

7

Harold Halley sat in his car in the farmland of Bakersfield, California. He wondered if Julia found his note on the refrigerator, an innocuous little note written with cowardice and very little guilt—but true—every word of it. He was on his way to Mexico. It was too hard to look at Nancy, and he had no money for her expensive medical bills.

He laid his head back on the seat. It was a hot summer day in the valley, and he soon went to sleep, only to be awakened by a little boy tapping on the car window. When he rolled it down he could smell the onion fields outside. It was sizzling hot and his shirt was soaked with sweat. He had no water—only a half-bottle of whisky—and for the first time in many years it didn't appeal to him. He turned to ask the child for water but the youngster had disappeared. The white-hot sun stood high in the sky and the heat radiated in waves off the earth below.

Harold—by this time thoroughly disorientated and dehydrated—stayed in his car until the sun set, then opened the door and fell headfirst into the onion field where he was found dead the next morning. During the night vandals had relieved him of his wallet, stolen the car radio as well as the tires, and left him stretched on the ground with an empty bottle of Jack Daniels. The police identified him by his fingerprints, notified Julia who used the remaining funds in their bank account to give him a cheap burial in Bakersfield. He would never have to lay eyes on Nancy again. Julia hated him.

At San Francisco General Hospital, Julia put her arms around Nancy explaining that her father had been away on business and driven off the road and died. She substantiated this half-truth to herself with the knowledge that he had driven off the road a long time ago—only this time he never got back on. Nancy loved Harold, as Harold was the only father she had ever known, and his negligence had never been augmented with abuse. Best let her think the best. Alcohol is available everywhere on earth and sometimes the only successful cure for the habit, (addiction, need, disease whatever it's called) is the permanent cure—death. Harold was cured, he would never drink again.

In the San Francisco police interrogation room, detective Lennen listened to a derelict confessing to the Crowl murder—a sorry looking individual well known in the seedier parts of town. The kind of man you would step over on the street while holding your nose. Perhaps he read about the murder of a lawyer in a cast off Chronicle he had picked up or slept on or under, and believed he had been the perpetrator of the deed during one of the many memory gaps in his besotted brain. Or perhaps, like he said, he had killed the man. He was able to furnish the correct information that the victim had been shot with a 38, although he was unable to say where it was. Inspector Lennen took down the information and in a number of weeks he would be tried and found guilty of the murder.

In South San Francisco, a lean pit bull slunk through a cemetery in the little town of Colma with its nose to the ground. He was hungry, having lived on a protein-free diet out of garbage cans for weeks now. King—that was his name—sniffed the ground but finding nothing to eat marched on, circumventing the gravestones he padded to the top of the hill where he lay down like a one-headed Cerebus guarding the entrance of an elaborately decorated stone mausoleum.

In San Francisco outside her daughter's room in San Francisco General Hospital, Julia Halley put her head down and cried when she received the news that she was not a compatible kidney donor for her daughter, Nancy Haley.

8

In Tiberon Margaret brought in the afternoon mail, there was a small note from Julia Halley (signed Nancy's mother) who wanted to see her, but was afraid to meet her that day at Spenger's restaurant. The note also included her phone number.

Margaret phoned that evening and they made arrangements to meet at Margaret's house the next day. She was sure now she would stay in her own home.

The following afternoon Margaret took small hesitant steps down the hallway before opening the front door as the doorbell rang. Julia had not changed from the time she had seen her eleven years ago. The memory of the sounds of the chiming clock came back so intensely it could have been coming from the next room. Looking at Julia, the fact that Sidney had been the Halley's attorney caused her to be a bit shaky. What had Julia told him? Had Sidney known about Nancy?

"Mrs. Crowl . . . your husband was my attorney—please accept my condolences—I am so sorry . . . I had no idea you were his wife until I saw your picture on his desk. Please—I think I need to talk with you, may I come in?"

Margaret stood still for a split second before she opened the door and invited her inside, "Please do." Once inside she led her to the balcony. "We can sit outside."

When they were seated Julia told Margaret how Nancy had grown up, and how the family moved to the Bay Area, then about Harold having died in an auto accident, etcetera. Throughout this long soliloquy, Margaret twisted in her seat but listened politely thinking she could have done without this information, why is she telling me all this? But then she sat forward with full attention when Julia started to cry, unfolding the real reason for the visit.

"I really need to talk with you about Nancy."

So. Margaret thought go on just tell me. She gripped the arms of her chair when Julia divulged Nancy's urgent need of a compatible kidney, and she was not a match for a transplant. Margaret had given up her claim to motherhood years ago, but this was as close as she would ever come to any maternal emotion. When Julia explained that if they couldn't find a match and the child might die, she heard herself saying in a voice that seemed to be coming far in the distance from someone else, "Of course, I'll be tested tomorrow."

Afternoon turned into evening, evening into darkness, and Julia found herself sleeping in the guest room after both women—now widows—had voiced their fears of loneliness. She liked Julia. She felt comfortable talking with her, in fact so comfortable that she was able to tell her neither her parents nor in-laws were aware that she had ever had a baby. Julia swore it would remain their secret. There was only one question she couldn't bring herself to ask Julia, and that was, "Did you tell Sidney I was Nancy's birth mother?" But now it didn't really matter, so instead she said, "I am sorry to hear about Mr. Halley—poor Nancy, and poor you. Let's go make some hot chocolate."

Julia agreed on all counts as she followed her into the kitchen.

9

Nancy was transferred to Children's Hospital in Oakland to await the kidney transplant. Her surgeon Dr. Levy was a tall kindly doctor who didn't seem at all surprised when the women explained their relationship. Margaret turned out to be the perfect match for the kidney transplant and the operation was over and completed within two days. After a couple of days in the hospital Margaret was home minus one kidney and Nancy was functioning fine with her new one.

Margaret didn't opt to visit Nancy, and told herself it was because she was still tired and the incision hurt. She wondered what Sidney would have thought, were he alive. She had no desire to see Nancy. She simply was not the motherly type, but Julia seemed so disappointed she agreed to go.

As she spoke to Nancy she felt a little twinge in her back over her missing kidney. "Hi Nancy, I'm a friend of your mother's."

She tried to keep the shock out of her voice when she looked at the child's mutilated face. Some of the bandages had been removed revealing healing red scars that would forever mar her flesh, but her eyes shone with hope as she looked up. Margaret wanted to touch her, but spoke instead. "I am happy to meet you young lady." After a few sentences about school and her pretty nightgown the two women left.

After a brief visit at the hospital the women went back to Tiberon where they sat on the balcony.

Margaret and Julia found it easy to talk to each other, even though they were as different as night and day. Margaret mourned the loss of her husband. Julia felt relief in the loss of hers. Margaret was financially well off while Julia was almost destitute, and would have to move as her house would soon be in foreclosure.

Margaret was now the sole owner of a home big enough for a large family, so when she invited Julia to temporarily move in, she readily accepted saying she would get a job and pay her way. Margaret was somewhat tired and sore from the surgery and Julia was proving to be a great help around the house. It seemed at times as if Julia considered the child a piece of her private property, always referring to her as "my child" as if she were fearful of losing ownership.

Helmet, Helene, Maurice and Janice did all they could do to comfort Margaret after the loss of Sidney, but none of them could figure out how she knew this Julia woman, nor why they were living together. In reply to Janice's questions Margaret answered in a simple offhanded manner, "Oh mom, I met her at a fund raiser." This seemed to do the trick, for her mother's questions then led the conversation to aid to the Lighthouse for The Blind and her volunteer work there.

Her parents had been at Lake Tahoe for three weeks, and when they returned she told them she had had a routine hysterectomy and there was no reason not to believe her. Her mother brought flowers to her and commented that this woman, Julia, had stayed with her for a long time. But she explained that away by telling her Julia did the cooking and cleaning, as she still felt weak from her surgery.

"But she is a perfect stranger, are you out of your mind?"

"You are right mother, completely crazy. Mom and Dad, I am tired, I think I'll go to bed. Let's talk tomorrow." And with that she guided them to the door. They had no choice but to leave.

Later when she was in bed with her eyes wide open, Margaret wondered about herself. Was it a protective maternal instinct buried in the female subconscious since the beginning of humankind? Who knows? She did realize after Sidney's death, somehow life had become more precious, for like a lighted match she saw that life could be blown out with only one breath. She couldn't save Sidney but she had saved Nancy. Maybe that's all it really was, just an inordinate fear of death. Anybody's and everybody's.

Not raised in any religion, neither a benevolent nor vengeful God worried her. An occasional visit to a church or temple for a wedding or funeral was the extent of her spiritual upbringing, although she could remember her grandmother had statues of the saints and prayed the rosary. She wished she could have that kind of faith. To be able to pray must be a comforting ritual. To really believe in miracles or a God even more comforting. But even though she looked at modern miracles as being guided by the hands of science, she never quite lost the longing to believe there might be—just perhaps—a benevolent God behind today's modern scientific discoveries. Stretched out motionless in her lonely bed in the quiet and of her bedroom, she found herself looking into the darkness and praying.

Julia could not thank her enough and this was beginning to get on Margaret's nerves. She resented Julia's obsequious manner, almost bowing double in reverence like a Japanese housemaid as she followed her around the house. It was time for Julia to leave. Julia was feeling it, too. The women had both rallied to save Nancy, but Julia had started to show indications of jealousy. One day, out of the blue, she turned to Margaret and said, "If Nancy ever learns what you did for her she will love you more. I know I can never be her real mother. Maybe you shouldn't visit her so often. She might learn who you really are."

Margaret stopped peeling the potatoes as she watched the monster jealousy loom its ugly head in Julia's demeanor, and somewhat angry without thinking she quickly responded, "Maybe I should not visit her at all. Julia, I told you that she would never—and I mean never—hear that from me. What more can I say." Neither of them said anything after that.

The afternoon silence was interrupted by the doorbell. An almost cloudless sky hung over a bay dotted with little white sailboats creeping smoothly across the ocean. A monarch butterfly landed on the railing but soon flew away—a cat was climbing a tree at the end of the yard. The two women sat in silence on the terrace, each with a glass of wine. It was late afternoon and Margaret set her wine glass on the floor next her chair when the doorbell rang.

"I need the exercise Julia, I'll get it." The real reason was that she wanted to answer her own front door.

When she opened the door Margaret found herself looking into the eyes of a youngish woman holding a newspaper in one hand. The woman wore thick horned-rimmed glasses—a long brown skirt nearly reached her sensible brown oxfords. A loose fitting khaki jacket over a grey turtleneck sweater topped the incongruous outfit. Her mousy hair was held in a ponytail by a thick rubber band. As she was neat and clean the first thing Margaret thought was, I bet she is some kind of Missionary.

"Yes?" she queried.

Meanwhile Julia had walked up behind her and gave a surprised little yelp followed by, "Little Cindy, is that really you?"

"None other. I got back from the Gold Coast and learned from the lady across the street from where you used to live and what had happened. She showed me a clipping from the paper and I pulled a few strings and found you. I am so sorry. What a perfectly terrible thing for Nancy" Julia reached her hands out circumventing Margaret to lead Cindy inside and introduced them. "This is my little sister Cindy."

Greetings were exchanged, but Margaret was stuck on the ensemble of so many articles of mismatched clothing, marveling that despite all this the girl still looked pretty!

"Cindy had been in the Peace Corps on the Gold Coast in Africa." Slowly nodding, for she was still processing the ensemble, Margaret didn't realize it but it had tweaked her memory back to the days in the Haight. Gathering her wits she invited her to join them on the terrace.

Cindy could not have shown up at a better time, and over glasses of Chardonnay the sisters decided they would live together and make a home for Nancy. It never came to light just who Margaret really was, other than the widow of the attorney who had been helping the Halley's with the dog bite suit.

Margaret went to the hospital only once with Julia and Cindy, but deemed it wise to wait in the hall. She was relieved to hear that the kidney transplant had taken and Nancy was out of danger. Julia and had decided before the transplant that it would be less traumatic for Nancy at this time to convalesce without knowledge of the adoption. When the time came, it would be up to Julia to tell her or not. Right now, losing a father and learning that her mother was not her real mother—to say nothing of being ripped into shreds by a dog and losing a kidney—would be just too much for any child.

Aunt Cindy was a godsend, for she offered to watch Nancy while her mother was working in the school cafeteria right next to the small cottage they had rented outside the Castro district.

When the sisters were settled they said goodbye to Margaret. They each gave Margaret a hug at her front door, after which the women would never see each other again—nor did she ever expect to see Nancy again. Margaret stepped back into her empty house but she wasn't as sad as she expected. A sense of tranquility came over her. She needed to be alone. The telephone was ringing. She picked it up. Oh Lord, it was her mother inviting her to lunch.

"Sorry mom, I have an appointment with the manicurist can we make it next Thursday?"

"Sure thing, Dad and I will come over tonight after dinner anyway. Glad that poor girl, whatever her name was, and the other strange thing moved out. You are so thoughtful to have taken them in like that—I guess your dad and I did something right when we raised you. You are certainly a great help to the needy. Oh well, we can talk tonight." After saying goodbye to her mother she took an angel food cake out of the freezer.

That night, after Margaret made the coffee, she stood in the kitchen with her hand resting on the small scar on her stomach over her missing kidney; it was beginning to itch, a sure sign of healing. The doorbell rang. Expecting her parents, she dropped her hand and turned up the corners of her mouth into a smile on the way to the front door.

"Hi Mom and Dad. The coffee is ready. Let's sit on the terrace and look at the view. As tomorrow is Mother's Day and you are the only mother around here, I'll bring out the cake and coffee and you can have the honor of cutting it Mom—Happy Mother's Day."

Thou Shalt Not

Northern England, 1196

A little mouse squeaked when Colette stepped on its tiny grey tail. Jumping aside she picked up her broom and gently but swiftly guided it into its hole in the wall. As it disappeared she was glad it was safe but spoke to it in words that came out harsher than she had intended.

"Keep out ye little gree rot."

Then walking across the room she muttered something about cleaning up dust being one thing but droppings another, although she didn't quite put it in those words. Her Mistress wouldn't permit harm to come to any of God's creatures so Colette carefully swept around four remaining spiders a small toad and a lizard lounging on the floor.

A wren flew in the window, circled around and flew out. It was spring and the birds were nesting, so occasionally one came in hunting for a bit of building material. In the tree outside, a nest was in progress containing bits of straw, familiar scraps of wool and discarded threads from the house. Birds were much more to her liking than anything that crawled. She even preferred the goose outside which bit her backside when she crossed its path.

She remembered the time two years ago when she had stepped on a fat brown spider about the size of a plum, its mucus-like innards squishing out all over the floor. Gagging she had to look up at the ceiling and think of something else while she scraped it up. Leaving work that day she had a great desire to run away but thought of her poor mum alone in their tiny cottage at the bottom of the hill depending on her for care and food, and thanked God she had the job. Mistress Marjorie would undoubtedly have said a prayer for that spider had she known.

But now the Mistress, a pretty round faced dark haired Yorkshire woman, a bit on the pleasingly plump side, was calling the young maid into her bedroom to help unclasp a necklace from around her neck. Colette unlatched it with ease and handed it to her. Looking at it pensively she held it in her hand before she turned to Colette.

"Thank you so much, this was my dear mothers. My father gave it to her. He had it made by a gold smith in Paris." She held it tenderly to her lips for a moment before continuing. "My mother gave it to me just before she died. May she rest in peace." Closing her eyes she crossed herself.

Colette looked at a gold chain holding a medallion set with a large diamond and two pearls.

"It are lovely ma'am."

"Yes" Marjorie nodded as she put it on the tall wooden clothes chest beside her bed and left the room.

Her work done, Colette took leave after the Mistress had given her a bowl of warm stew to take to her mother. Her brown curly hair fell in waves around her heart shaped face, her light blue eyes were cast downwards as she carefully guarded her steps along the uneven road grasping the bowl gingerly in her work worn hands.

It was almost dark when she opened the door of the cottage and found her mother wrapped in a woolen shawl sitting by a few dying embers of an almost cold fire. Coming up beside her mother, Colette bent down to show her the stew.

"Oh Mum, I'll poke up the fire and get yer some supper, will only be a minute. I'll warm up of this 'ere nice stew the Mistress sent yer."

The old lady didn't move and when Colette touched her arm she fell to the floor with a thud, her shawl still clinging around her shoulders. She was dead. The bowl in Colette's hands fell to the ground and like her mother lay spilled and cold on the floor.

Colette's father Dan, the carpenter, had been killed by a Saracen in Jerusalem in the holy crusade and thus his entrance into Heaven—her father's that is—was guaranteed. This was a blessing, probably more to her father than her poor mother who was left a widow with two young children to look after. Her mother had found work as a serving woman in a local ale house for three months until a cough left her too weak to work. Colette was nine at the time so when the Mistress of the Ellington estate at the top of the hill needed a housemaid she began working there. Rudy, her little brother, died the following year and her mother had said it was because there wasn't enough fuel for the fire, but comforted herself by proclaiming it was God's will that he be with his father. Now, she too had left this world leaving Colette alone.

The girl stood in the cold room and flung her hands skyward.

"Holy Mother of God what am I to do?"

And then she decided. She would leave the little village of Wath-upon-Dear in Northern England, leave her work on the hill, and look for her mother's sister Olivia, wife of Tom the Inn keeper of The Three Roses, in London. Her father had no living relatives in Scotland that she knew about and the only stories she remembered her father telling her, when she was just eye-level to the hatchet he wore tucked in his belt, was how the Campbell's fought anybody and everybody but mostly among themselves. No she trod with fear of the Scots. It was best she head for London.

She buried her mother next to her little brother before sun up the next morning, and left the same day. Her shoes were almost worn through, her coat was threadbare, but her spirit willing. She could never tell her mistress that she had trouble with the crawling creatures or that she was mainly uncomfortable with the way the master looked at her, even running his hand over her body when the mistress wasn't looking, no, no—it was easier to just run away.

After burying her mother, she stole up to the manor house, crept silently in through the back entrance and took some of the Masters clothes. She would put them on just before leaving. He was short man and by luck they wore nearly the same size. She took an uninvited louse or two with his undergarments and tucked a couple of his tunics under her arm before wending her way back down the hill. It was almost full daylight when she got home, cut her hair, put on the Master's pants, donned a clean tunic and walked away from Wath as a young boy.

Colette shivered, it was spring but the weather was still cold. After two days on the road her shoes were completely worn through and had she not met the robust man and full bodied woman on horseback with a donkey pulling their covered cart she would have had to stop walking. They were probably thieves but as she had nothing to rob, they were of no threat, and actually the presence of a young boy completed their image of a family so they were delighted when she agreed to travel with them. She joined not only the couple but a cart full of stolen goods. Riding in the cart until her feet were healed gave her time to go through the candlesticks, silver plates, cutlery, jewelry, fine linens and tapestries jiggling along with her. The man called himself Tom and the woman called herself Marion. She chose the name Anthony for herself.

It became her job to go on ahead into the hamlets, put on a pathetic face, not difficult, to beg for food. Some villagers were generous enough to feed the whole family, but others were not. One time a tall thin man wielding a stick ran toward the cart demanding to see what was inside and when Marion told him it was the bodies of their two little sons who had died of the pox Colette looked back just in time to see him trip, fall and drop the stick in his haste to escape.

With Tom as her father and Marion as her mother and she as Anthony they made their way to London begging and stealing. Just outside the forest of Nottingham Tom and Marion managed to steal a box from a lone rider, that turned out to be filled with jewelry seemingly worth a king's ransom They had never killed anyone, or so they said, so Colette learned to tolerate, in fact to embrace, her life as a highwayman. If she had found out they were murderers, as so many robbers were, she planned to leave immediately. Perhaps those years of not even killing so much as a flea had rubbed off on her, making a human killing seem even more frightful. Being so short she could continue to pass for a young boy, but it was a blessing when she found a baggy old coat along the roadside that she could wear to cover her developing breasts.

*   *   *

The day when Colette failed to show up as she was burying her mother, Marjorie went into the large sitting room, on the east side of the house. Roger sat at a table holding a silver bowl in his hands, a two-handled bowl about the size for a single serving of soup, He held it up, close to his eyes, scrutinizing the relief figures interspersed with scrolls. After wielding a rock and killing the tottering old man on his return trip from business in London, he had picked it up from the priest's belongings. Now putting the bowl down, he moved uneasily on the chair when he heard the door open. There were papers spread out in front of him and a scattering of silver coins midst the clutter. He looked up as Marjorie spoke

"Roger, have you seen Colette? The dogs barked early this morning. I thought I heard somebody in the house, I peeked out in the hall but nobody was there. Colette should be here any minute and she can look around. I hope her mother is well. I sent her some stew yesterday. Where is that girl? Roger! Roger!" When Roger only shrugged his shoulders and didn't answer his wife she turned and left the room.

After Marjorie brought him his morning tea, he told her he must go to York again this very day on business. He saddled a fast horse and was gone before noon, but returned late the next day.

When Colette failed to appear at the end of the second day, Marjorie sent a servant down to the village to learn that mother and daughter were gone, simply nowhere to be found.

A week later Marjorie ran her hand across the top of her tall wooden chest feeling for her necklace. She remembered Colette helping her open the clasp and taking it off, then handing it to her, and she remembered putting it back on the top of the chest. It was not there. She pulled the chest away from the wall got down on her hands and knees to search behind it and then looked in all of the drawers. It was gone!

As people do, she immediately thought someone had taken it. Most likely Colette, as she had admired it so much. Had Colette stolen it and then left with her mother? A possibility! She often left jewelry on the chest and Colette had never touched it before. Only this one time when the clasp was stuck. Hmm, she had admired it. Oh, where had that girl gone? If she hadn't stolen it wouldn't she have said good-bye?

Marjorie looked for her other jewelry in the box on her dressing room table. It too was gone, box and all. This led her to conclude without a doubt that Colette had robbed her, for who else besides Roger would know where she kept her jewels.

Before the end of the month, Roger lent Colette's house to a newlywed couple with the agreement that the young bride, Nancy, would take Colette's place.

Nancy, a big strong beefy well-rounded girl of 17, with a slight limp but a more noticeable stutter agreed to preserve all life, although the spiders annoyed her. The little mouse was now busy with its own family of 9 little mice. There was also a nest of young wrens outside the window that would soon become fledglings and leave. Nancy thought of bringing a snake into the house to eliminate the mice, but then she really couldn't do it in all good conscience, as the little mice seemed so precious to the Mistress. Maybe they took the place of children? Oh well, best she not question that subject. Besides, Nancy would have her own baby in six months and her poor mistress would still have only the nest of little mice, if that, as they would be all grown up by then. She thought about telling her about the witch in the next village with an herb and a charm for barren women, but then thought better of it.

*   *   *

After a leisurely trip from Yorkshire, a donkey, two horses and a set of foster parents with a little boy in baggy clothing approached London, the hub of England, a city of around 1,800 people.

When they were about two hours away in a densely wooded Oak forest they encountered their last victim, a lone man on horseback, dozing in the saddle. Draped behind the saddle were two bulging leather bags that caught Tom's eye and quick as a wink he steered his horse behind the rider, hit him over the head and absconded with both bags with the greatest dexterity Colette had ever seen, leaving the rider with little more than a raging headache. When Colette crept up to the victim her mouth fell open in disbelief. It was Roger, her master! She quickly lowered her head before Tom or Marion could notice, her shocked look but her skinny little legs felt like jelly. When they opened the saddlebags it was the Mistresses jewelry; but Anthony never told "his parents." Why did the Master have it? Could Marjorie have died? Suddenly Colette felt sick.

The following day they rode up to the walls of London a drifting family of tired travelers with an equally tired old grey donkey pulling an old covered cart. She thought of her mother and the aunt she had never seen. An Aunt Olivia living somewhere in London—what would she ever tell her, if she found her? Of course, she might even be dead and that would save telling her about her niece being a thief, a liar and not really a boy.

In London they found themselves surrounded by people— merchants selling everything from apples to pork pudding, lace, ribbons and buttons. The smell of damp wool hung heavy in the air outside stores where shorn wool was piled high in woven straw baskets. Stores displaying woolen materials were nearby and local farmers stood by carts piled high with fruit and vegetables. Midst all of these activities were urchins, dressed mostly like Anthony, dodging here and there with their little hands out begging. Most were so adept at the game of 'cut purse' they could snatch a person's moneybag right off his body before he even knew it. London was not terribly large but was terribly busy and Colette looked around in amazement. How could she ever find Aunt Olivia?

The houses were made of wattle and daub and the stores mostly of just plain wooden planks. She looked up and down the street. Perhaps she should just knock on all the doors asking for the wife of the Innkeeper of The Three Roses. But then quick as a wink, Tom grabbed her by the shoulder digging his thumb into her neck and dragged her through a front door into the back of one of the stores. There was a square table in the center of the room and a wall behind with an open door to the outside. As quickly as Tom pulled Roger off of his horse he now pulled Colette into the store his strong hand forcing her down on her knees. This was not a welcome she expected. There were two scruffy men standing by the table heaped high with the contents of the cart. Jewels glistened and gleamed as Tom sifted through them with his pudgy fingers. Outside the cart and donkey were visible through the open door at the back and the two horses were tied to a post next to the stile nearby. Colette sat silently on the floor rubbing the shoulder that Tom had used to propel her to the floor. She was just eye-level to the tabletop, the room smelled of unwashed bodies that all seemed to be talking at once.

She didn't pay a great deal of attention until she heard Marion say, "Ow much you give me for the boy?" She was looking at Colette, who straightened up and declared mostly from fear of course, "I am not for sale—I come to see me aunt."

One of the men looked at her with tiny bloodshot eyes peering out from under black bushy eyebrows before he turned to Marion with a look of disgust, "Marion for God's sake shut up, I don't want no boy. This one is too skinny anyway. Now if he were a gir…?" His eyes squinted even more lecherously as he let out a long burst of laughter, followed by an even longer rolling fart.

Just then a corpulent man burst into the room puffing, wheezing and belching his way to the table. From Colette's vantage point on the floor he looked all belly.

"Awright, let's see what yer got. I don't have all day." He pulled out a wrinkled silk cloth that was draped over a woven fiber belt encircling his enormous girth and blew his nose and then proceeded to wipe the sweat from his face along with the spittle that had escaped through the many gaps in his teeth and lay in little rivulets clinging to his chin. Tucking the cloth back under his belt he cocked his head to one side, for he could only see out of one eye, and took one enormous stride to the table where all the occupants had gathered like flies on the dead. All except Colette. She seized the opportunity and was out the backdoor, over the stile, and up the hill before Mr. Spittle could spit out another word.

She ran until her lungs ached, then fell exhausted in the tall grass and listened. No one had followed so she relaxed, gasped and let out a breath of gratitude.

For the next two days, she managed to live in the back alleys of London stealing or begging for food and dodging the slops thrown from the windows. A myriad of smells met her nostrils at every turn. Cabbage vied with fried potatoes, garbage mixed with human waste sent up its own odor, the acrid smell of ale wafted out from the alehouse and all these ingredients were highly seasoned with the broth of unwashed bodies.

She feared the robbers might be looking for a runaway boy, so with the aid of a long skirt and shift as well as a drab head scarf grabbed off of a drying line she dropped the louse ridden clothes of Anthony in a smoldering unattended fire. Shaking out her curly hair she twisted it into individual curls, darkened her eyebrows with charcoal and tied the scarf around her head. Nobody looked twice at her. The boy who had entered London had vanished.

There was a scary moment though when she almost rubbed shoulders with Marion in a back alley as she walked past the cart. She clenched her jaws and mumbled at her under her breath, "Sell me indeed, no! Ya ugly ole woman. A pox on ye."

A few days later while making her way down a busy street she looked up, unable to believe her eyes. There was Master Roger with his arm around this young tart wearing clothing at least one size too small. Both were awfully drunk, weaving, and stumbling every which way. Colette cringed and tried to make herself smaller but soon realized that even had she looked him straight in the eye he was beyond recognizing her, and probably would have seen two of whatever he saw. It was then, when the tart stumbled and bumped up against her that she saw the Mistress's necklace around her neck. She blinked in astonishment. However, there it was, circling her skinny neck. In utter amazement, she got behind the happy couple and followed them into the nearest alehouse where they stumbled to a table and the tart proceeded to pat him like dog in heat while the diamond in the necklace moved in rhythm on top of a throbbing artery on her throat.

Roger was talking in slurred words.

"There my lil' beauty. Do you like your necklashe? I bought it jus fur you." He put his greedy little palm on her breast and reached inside her blouse to finger her nipple as she fingered the big diamond. They drank more.

Colette sitting bent over at a nearly table and raised one charcoaled eyebrow in disgust.

When a buxom barmaid all smiles asked what she wanted she gave her a wink and asked her to come back in a minute, cuz her man was just outside. It was then she decided she would follow Lady Tart outside when she went to relieve herself, which should be soon figuring the amount of ale she had been drinking, She would exercise her skill as a highway robber and get the necklace for she certainly knew how the clasp worked!!

Sure enough, the tart soon excused herself and stumbled toward the backdoor. Colette followed. They both ended standing over the dirt just across the path from the alehouse. The stench was awful and the tart almost fell in the single hole in the ground but Colette smiled and stepped forward and offered a hand to help her. Putting one hand under her arm to right her she slipped the other around her neck, opened the clasp and had the necklace off before 'Her Tartship' could finish her business.

Clasping the necklace she hid behind a tree and couldn't help but think, Tom would have been proud of me but Ol' Marion would have upped me selling price. She watched the tart stumble back inside oblivious to her loss. As she stepped out from behind the tree a sour faced old man either blind or drunk or both bumped her aside. She would pretend she was with the old man if anyone came after her, but no one followed. It was getting dark and fearful to stay in the area she followed close behind the old man, who turned off at the next turn in the road. Exhausted she went straight ahead putting one foot in front of the other until she reached a blacksmith shop, spied a pile of hay behind the building and plopped down in it where she slept through the night with the necklace clutched in her hand. When the early morning sun woke her she jumped up quickly, washed her face in the horse trough, went to the privy behind the shop and walked out to the road. She was covered with bits of straw and terribly hungry.

She asked the first man she passed on the street, maybe the blacksmith, although he really looked too clean for that trade, if he knew where she could find The Inn of The Three Roses? He pointed down the road.

"I think so but to make sure I'll ask my friend at that inn over there, he knows about everybody in London"

The man was young and kind and clean and just a pinch this side of handsome and the fact that Colette was disheveled and covered with straw did not preclude him from acting like a gentleman. She waited outside the Alehouse as he enquired inside and soon came back with the information that it was just over the next hill and right next to the shop of Martin the Meat Seller.

Turning to Colette he said, "Just keep walking straight ahead." Colette must have looked frightened as she explained that she didn't know London very well, so he took her hand, the one without the necklace, and offered to show her. She would never forget what happened next.

*   *   *

Back in Wath, Roger had been gone for three weeks after telling the mistress he was going to London to arrange something about buying a warehouse to store wool. Now, back from London, he rode through Wath and up to his estate early in the evening of a Saturday. Marjorie never had quite known his holdings. She was also ignorant of the fact that Roger had been stealing money from her dowry for years to pay debts and support an excessive self-indulgent lifestyle in London. Over the years he had lost his entire estate to gambling debts. Nor did she know that before his last trip to London he had stolen her jewelry with the intention of selling it. Nor that on his way home he had waylaid a priest whose only possession was the silver bowl. He sat at his desk now examining this priceless antique fashioned in Roman times to the goddess Venus. Roger did not particularly like to steal from a priest and Marjorie would have died on the spot, but he was so desperate he relieved the old priest of the bowl, put it in a sack and threw it over the back of his horse. Now he wondered just what it might be worth. Probably nothing, but he would take it to London and sell it to old Sam the Innkeeper.

He thought back on his sojourn in London. Roger was never happier than when he was lavishing expensive gifts on greedy London prostitutes who inflated his ego in proportion to the size of the gift. Before he had left the latest gift presented itself to him on top of Marjorie's tall wooden chest, and as he had already packed Marjorie's jewels in his saddlebags, he tucked the necklace into his riding boot.

Now back home when Marjorie met Roger at the door with news of her missing jewelry her husband met the news with pretended surprise. At supper Roger promised her another necklace next time he went to London. He ran his eyes up and down Nancy, blooming with the beauty of early pregnancy while licking his lips as he commented on the delicious pheasant. Marjorie watched him with disdain as they ate in silence.

*   *   *

In London not far from a blacksmith shop, Colette and the boy walked to the Inn of the Three Roses. The sun was almost straight overhead when they reached it. They walked into a wooden building that smelled of ale but almost bereft of people, which made it quiet at this time of day. Colette's eyes took a little while to adjust from the bright sunlight outside to the comparative darkness inside and it was a few minutes before she could focus her eyes on the woman who was walking across the room toward them, but when she did she fainted dead away. The next thing she remembered was waking up on a little sofa in a sitting room with the woman looking down at her. The woman had turned to the young man who had brought her and it seemed they were discussing her.

"No ma'am, I don't know who she is. She asked me directions to this inn, so I offered to bring her." The woman had a puzzled look on her face.

"Did she tell you her name, or where she is from? She is thin as a bird this girl"

As Colette was awake now she answered the question.

"Me name is Colette from Yorkshire. Me mum told me she 'ad a sister in London. Me father died in the crusade and me mum just died, so I…" Her voice cracked and tears sprang to her eyes before she could continue, So I come to London." she hesitated then looked hopefully at the lady bending over her as she said in a whisper, "You must be mum's sister, Olivia? You look exactly like me mum.

She took a deep breath before she continued. "I do good housework. I worked for a lady in Wath for four years," and then her mouth went dry when she looked down at her hands and realized the necklace was gone. The boy who had brought her was gone too. He had walked out of the door when he heard she was in the right place.

Olivia sat down on the edge of the sofa and looked at Colette, kindly but with apprehension, she said, "Oh, my poor twin. Yes, I am Olivia. Please don't look so frightened Colette—you may stay here. What is the matter child you're white as milk? How about some hot mutton broth and then we can talk." She turned around and went to the kitchen.

"Thank you ma'am, er I mean Aunt Olivia?"

While Olivia was in the kitchen, Colette's eyes spotted a grey kitten playing with something shiny in a dark corner. A little patch of sun light sparkled on the diamond. God be thanked. She jumped up and retrieved the necklace just seconds before Olivia came back with the broth. Raising the bowl to her lips she drank it all. Never had a bowl of broth tasted so good. Olivia was staring at her quizzically.

"That's a good girl, you look better already"

Colette handed her the empty bowl and then looked around. She was in a lovely sitting room, with beautiful paintings decorated the walls, paintings that she couldn't take her eyes off. One looked just like a picture owned by the master and mistress hanging in their estate in Yorkshire—the painting of a young child sitting at the feet of the Virgin. She hesitated before she asked, "Aunt do yer live here by yerself?"

As if to answer her question, a large man burst in the door speaking in a booming voice as he drew a filthy rag from under his tunic, blew his nose and looked around the room with his one good eye.

"Roger, that weasel from Wath, is in London today. He came into the inn a little while ago saying he was robbed on the way. What he doesn't know is that Old Tom the Quick Sword was the robber. I seen the takings in town meself! Ol' Tom was describing some of the very things Roger brought to the store, almost to a stickpin. Ha ha. Poor ole Roger, he is down to nothing and damned if I'll help him, the cheating rat. Olivia where's the ale? I've had a hard morning. Oh, oops, I didn't see that child sitting there. Hello, and who are we?" He stepped across the room, tilted his grubby head and looked at Colette right in the face with unabashed curiosity.

"And what's yer name, little girl?" She watched him wipe his nose and run the well-used rag over his face smearing the spittle as it continued to run down through the holes between his teeth. Shaking she stood up trying to inch herself out of the sunlight. She turned to Olivia and said with obvious desperation.

"Please ma'am may I run outside, I need to, and she clenched her teeth as she rubbed her hand over her belly?"

"Of course child," said Olivia pointing to the back door.

Tightly clutching the necklace she curtsied as she backed across the room and fled out through the door. Running as fast as she could, down first one street and then another until breathless she came to what must have been the edge of town for there was a wide river. Tied to the bank was a little riverboat all covered with some sort of fiber like material so she slid under it, and hid in the belly of the boat.

After lying quietly for what seemed like an eternity and when she was sure she didn't hear anyone she peeked out from under the covering into the twilight. The moon was just coming up. The river was a deep indigo. Church bells were ringing. She climbed out of the boat, turning her ankle as she slipping down the bank. It was here behind St Bartholomew's church that the old priest found her limping in pain.

"Young mistress do you have a home? It is dangerous to be out alone after eventide. Are you lost? My name is Father Mathew." She was shivering and limping for by now the pain was almost unbearable. She told him her name and then the whole story. You don't lie to a priest, as he can send you right to hell so she told him the truth. She didn't want to go to hell with all the Saracens for she knew for sure her father would be in heaven and her mother too so she even revealed the story of the diamond necklace and how she had stolen it from that Tart's neck. She was quite exhausted when she finished. The kindly priest just shook his head.

"Come with me Mistress, we will go see the Mother Superior at the convent. It's right over here next to the church. Just a few more steps." As she limped along in pain he said with compassion,

"I know your ankle must hurt. Here take my arm" The Mother Superior is a nurse so she will help you."

The Mother Superior bandaged her ankle assuring her it was only swollen not broken. That night she ate in the priory kitchen and slept in the infirmary. The nuns said a special prayer at matins for she had told Mother Clarissa about her father being a crusader and losing his life in Jerusalem as well as the story of the necklace she clutched in her hand. Mother Clarissa agreed to keep the necklace safely locked in a box until Colette could return it.

She felt peaceful, safe and loved in the convent where she stayed about a month until she could walk again.

One evening, weeks later, The Mother Superior called her into her office.

"Colette what are you planning to do now that you are well? I understand you have no honest Christian family."

"Mother Clarissa I don't know. I fear me uncle, and I fear Master Roger or ever even seeing the Master or the mistress, I must find work. Mother Superior can I become a nun?"

"No, my child, not at this time as you would be doing it out of fear and as a means of escape. Later when you have returned the necklace as you know you must and are at peace with yourself it will be time to think about it again."

She knew Mother Clarissa was right but knew little else so she went into the chapel to pray for an answer, and in the next week when Mother Clarissa learned about the fifteen-year-old Widow of Derek the chicken farmer who needed a housemaid. It was ideal for Colette so she moved in with the widow, and would stay the winter until the snows were over and roads to the north less ominous. There was something comforting about reaching under a soft hen for a warm egg.

$$*\qquad*\qquad*$$

When spring came and the leaves once again adorned the trees and as the snow had melted she knew what she must do. She made plans to return to Wath with the necklace. Almost as a way of accommodating Collette, the old lady died. Collette left it in God's hands as to what she could tell Mistress Marjorie.

Father Michael made arrangements for her to travel with a band of Irish Gypsies going to Yorkshire. There would be a young man assistant to the Bishop also going to enquire about a Cathedral being built in the town of York. While the Gypsies were thieving rascals, he knew a young girl would be safe under the auspices of the Church. She packed her meager belongings, said good-bye to Fr. Michael and the sisters, then left and waited by the gate.

The wagons arrived and Colette jumped in the middle one with the children. She thought of the birds and even the mice at the beautiful estate and hoped the Mistress would understand why she had left. How many times she had run away from things! Maybe it was good to run away. Maybe the Mistress should have run away from the Master. One had to decide what to run away from. Maybe Aunt Olivia should have run away, too. She would often think of that brief acquaintance with her Aunt but the fear of her barnyard pig of a thieving husband precluded any thoughts of ever returning. However, now the horses were pawing the ground and she must get started.

This time she was not running away but back and it could be just as frightening to know where you were headed as to not know where you were going.

A young man walked toward them. He wore the robes of a cleric's assistant and carried a breviary and when he got closer she realized he was the same young man who had taken her to find her Aunt Olivia. After he climbed into the last wagon all eight horses, four wagons and a great assortment of jangling pots and pans, a group of Gypsies and noisy children plus a young cleric, and a housemaid left London. Colette clutched the necklace in her left hand, which she rested on her lap under her right hand as if that hand were crippled, and nobody thought to ask about it.

The weather was fair. At night the gypsies slept under the wagons, the old women and young children inside. Colette often found a secluded spot away from the others. The young man smiled at her once, but she didn't think he remembered her.

During the nine days it took to reach York she liked being with the children. She had them laughing, singing and playing games along the way.

One evening the young assistant came over and sat beside her wagon. Turning to her he asked, "Why are you going to York Miss, do you have family there?"

"Oh no Sir I am going back to me home in Wath to see me former Mistress. What is your name Sir?" She did not think he remembered her.

"My name is Michael. I hope your hand will feel better soon. That hand in your lap."

*   *   *

The Caravan let her off at Wath but there was no answer after she made her way up to the estate and knocked on the kitchen door, waited and then knocked again. Everything was just too quiet. The door was ajar so she gathered her courage and walked inside. It was cold and as she made her way through the rooms looking around in amazement she saw how many things were missing, even the beautiful painting of the Virgin. Yes, now she was sure. Poor Aunt Olivia. She hoped her mother had never known the true story of her sister's life. She opened the door to the storeroom where the mouse had lived, the floor still covered with straw and the insect population roaming about unheeded. Quickly shutting the door behind her she slowly left and walked down the hill, feeling like 100 years had passed since she had last taken that walk. She was thankful Rodger was not there, but mostly concerned where Mistress Marjorie could have gone. She felt for the necklace still sewn in her aprons pocket with the thread one of the gypsy women had given her. When the wagons had stopped just before she reached Wath, on a pretext of a the call of nature she had sequestered herself behind a tree and sewn the necklace securely into a deep pocket where it hit her leg every time she walked; an assurance of its safe lodgings.

Soon Colette found herself turning left at the fork in the road just like she used to do and without thinking ended up in front of her old house. Peeking in the window there was a fire in the grate so she knocked. A young woman holding a baby opened the door.

"I am Colette I once lived in this house 'ad yer job too.

"Oh yes, the m-mistress told me. P-please come in. M-my name is Nancy.

After a short exchange of social pleasantries and the proper enthusiastic admiration of the baby, Nancy told her about the Ellington's. Poor Nancy stuttered so much, mostly m's and b's, that it was hard to follow her but Colette sat on the edge of her chair in rapt attention.

Nancy began by telling her all about the little animals in the house, and finally came to the missing necklace and the jewelry.

"The m-mistress was very upset about the necklace. And there was a jewelry b-box gone too" Colette just nodded as Nancy continued.

The Master said that he was sure that if anybody stole the things the dogs would have barked." Nancy went on

"Once the m-m-master turned to the m-m-mistress and said to her, M-M-Marjorie you walk in your sleep you might have t-taken the jewelry yourself." Colette becoming increasingly impatient interrupted her at this point

"But where are they now, nobody's there?"

She went on to explain in length how hard it was for the mistress after the Master had lost all his money and had to go to London, but explained that the Mistress, like a good wife should, accompanied him, pretending to her husband that she wanted to go too, she left with him.

Nancy was not hesitant to tell her about her work at the estate. Even the time the Master pushed her up against the wall and pinched her. She excused him because he was drunk, but not before she pinched him back and he threw some sort of a silver bowl at her, grazing the side of her head. She pointed to a small scar on her forehead and then pointed to the silver bowl on a small table in the corner. It had a dent in it so she had picked it up and took it home to show her husband. The next day was the day the Mistress and Master left in such a hurry and she could never return it.

All Colette could say was "Oh" and all she could think was the poor mistress, I wonder what she knows? She stood up.

"Well, I'll be on me way". She ended her visit giving Nancy a hug, saying something about what a nice baby and they would have to get together again soon and then left with a wave goodbye. She continued on her way to the little town of Wath. It was getting dark.

She had a few silver coins the widow had given her in London so she would stay at the Sandygate Inn that night and then, well and then what? The necklace hit her leg as she walked down the road.

The following day after a fitful sleep and a much-needed bath she started walking toward York. A kind old gentleman with a cart full of coal gave her a ride for the last few miles.

She hoped to find Michael and find out if he were going to London soon so she could give him the necklace to take back to Father Mathew or perhaps the Mother Superior who might find the mistress there. She thanked the old man for the ride and walked to the center of town,

York had one small stone church and she found Michael at prayer there. Waiting for him to rise from his knees she requested just a few minutes of his time. Outside the doors she told him the whole story. He said he would take the necklace on his trip back to London and talk to the priest at St Bartholomew's. Colette looked up at Michael, and after reaching in her pocket broke the thread holding the necklace and put it in his hand.

"God help the Mistress. Oh Michael what do you think?" Michael shook his head.

"I don't know. Colette what are you going to do for yourself?" He looked at her hard and long before he continued,

"The children could use a teacher to help the sisters. Can you read? The church is going to build a large cathedral right here next to this little church. It would be ideal now for the children of York to have a school. You were so good with the gypsy children. Could you?

"Yes, me father taught me to read some and I learned me letters at the convent. I would awfully like to teach the children, I really would," and she started to cry.

"Don't cry Colette" He so wanted to put his arms around her, but knew better than to yield to this temptation, as he might never let her go.

That afternoon Michael talked to the parish priest and soon she was teaching singing to the young children of York, under the guidance of one of the sisters from the nearby convent of St. Claire's. She lived in a room behind the convent kitchen and helped in the refectory until she joined the order a year later. The years that followed would be the happiest of her life. She was 18 years-old when she went to York never to return to Wath. The following year Michael went back to London took his vow of celibacy and became a priest. They never met again.

When Michael returned to St. Bartholomew's in London he took the necklace wrapped in a clean linen cloth to Father Mathew, explaining that the lady who owned the necklace had left Wath and was probably in London. But the ensuing enquiries by the good priest as to the whereabouts of Marjorie, wife of Roger of Wath, were to remain fruitless, as it seemed nobody in London had ever heard of her.

*   *   *

Sally had been a loyal housekeeper for the aging Monsignor Mathew for ten years when he, having lived a full and productive life, passed away. When she was going through his things she came across a bulky linen package yellow with age and tied with a hefty knot. Opening it she found a necklace. That was all. A diamond snuggled between two pearls looked up at her from its gold disk and like a bolt of lightning, the sight of the necklace brought back a memory sequestered for years behind the memory of a girl who called herself Sally. She caught her breath and sat down on the nearest chair as her former life materialized in her memory.

She recalled the days when she was Marjorie, married to Roger Ellington, who became a besotted alcoholic, pauper, cheat, liar and thief, and ran with the worst criminal element in London. Then her memory took her to a back alley, hungry, sick, and at her wits end, to the man who slapped her hard on the side of her head and demanded at knifepoint the rings off her fingers. It was in that instant her instinct took over and before she knew what she was doing she grabbed the knife from his hand and pushed it into Rogers throat and as his blood flowed she fled. Her identity as Marjorie shut the door on her memory as she climbed up the first step of St Bartholomew's and she became Sally before she even reached the top stair.

Now ten years later, time snapped her back like a recoiling spring when she looked at the medallion and remembered her mother, her mother whose name was Sally. She held the necklace in her hand, crossed herself, walked to St Bartholomew's and put the necklace in the poor box on her way to confession where she confessed to stabbing her husband. As it was the last thing she remembered she could not tell the priest for sure if Roger was dead, just wounded, or still alive. She had no idea of the present year, to Marjorie it was yesterday and when the good father realized ten years of her life had passed without leaving her a single memory, he gave her absolution.

As Marjorie left the church that day she would once again work under the name of Sally and leave Marjorie behind and the necklace in the poor box.

Was she aware of whom she really had been? Did it matter to anyone? Did she know herself? Probably not.

Once back in the rectory she picked up her broom and started sweeping, she skillfully avoided one shiny lizard, two spiders and a small moth. For some reason she remembered hearing somebody somewhere say that it was a sin to kill one of God's creatures. Or maybe she had only read it somewhere.

Afterwards York 1220

On the dirt road in Yorkshire England, Sister Mary Francis led the school children by the beginning of the structure of York minister, which would be completed in 1472. A cathedral which would become the second largest Gothic Cathedral in northern Europe. But now, in 1220 she led them into a small wooden structure with a simple wooden altar decorated with pine boughs for the Christmas season. The children would sing at the evening Mass, beautiful holy songs in Latin—some of them written as early as 400 A.D. They had been practicing for weeks. They were early, so when all were seated they bowed their heads to ask the Baby Jesus to bless their homes. Sister Mary Francis thought of Wath, of her father and mother, her Aunt Olivia in London, and Mistress Marjorie and the master, where ever they were.

Christmas was a hard time to be without family, but for many years now her family had been her sisters in the convent. She remembered the Holy Father, Pope Innocent III, Monsignor Mathew and Father Michael with a prayer. Michael was the only man who had ever caused her heart to flutter, but that was a long time ago and only God would ever know.

That Christmas eve her candle blew out at midnight and she died quietly in her sleep. All that remains of her story is a tiny wooden plaque on the east wall of a small wooden building in the city of York, right next to what would become the first Cathedral in Northern England.

The words imprinted are, *In memory of Sister Mary Francis 1220 AD*. That is all.

Who Knows

It is evening. I lie back under the shade tree on the top of the hill awaiting judgment. Unable to concentrate I sit up and put my head in my hands and look down at the ground to ponder: what's to become of me? This thought comes to mind in so many situations; the child caught with his hand in the cookie jar, the banker caught with his hand in the till, the patient hearing the doctors' diagnosis, and last, but not least, the innocent or guilty awaiting judgment in this life or perhaps worse yet, the next. I look down on my freshly painted ranch house, sparkling blue swimming pool and manicured green lawn. I am unable to come up with any answer.

My eyes drift to the large Sycamore branch jutting out parallel to the ground ten feet above my head; a branch strong enough to carry the weight of a man at the end of a rope with a noose around his neck. The picture is so vivid I must move to the sunset side of the tree. Moving, however, does not alleviate my hanging thoughts. I stand up, walk down the hill, steal through the backdoor into the kitchen and up the stairs to write in my journal to try and sort out what has just happened. I turn to a fresh page and begin to write.

*　　　　*　　　　*

I have been married three years. Notice I don't say happily married, just married, perhaps properly married on the happy side would be the best description. I finished two years of junior college before I joined the Marines in World War 11, and served in the Pacific until the war ended. I saw action that still haunts my dreams. Returning to California I met my wife purely by chance in the Piggly Wiggly grocery store. I was captivated by her fetching smile, cute figure, and melodious voice. She could have been Doris Day. Introducing myself, we talked right there by the canned soup and made a date for that evening.

She told me she had worked in the shipyards during the war and we decided between the Navy and the home front, America was bound to win. We dated almost every night: dinner, movies, and even went a couple of times to fancy nightclubs so popular in the Los Angeles area. We laughed a lot. She was like a breath of spring. It was stylish to get married and live happily ever after and reside on an Elm or a Cedar Street so we opted to try our hand at it. We had known each other for only a month but the euphoria at the end of the war and the propaganda offered through the movies with the happily-ever-after endings convinced us. We drove out of state to Nevada and got married at a chapel in Reno with two strangers standing up for us. It didn't seem important that she had never mentioned any friends or acquaintances.

She really did look like Doris Day with her short blond hair trim figure and infectious smile so I opted for the role of Rock Hudson, She wore cute cotton house dresses, cooked Tamale Pie from scratch and could sing, too. I can just see her in the kitchen in a frilly white starched apron holding a wooden spoon and stirring a casserole while humming the latest song maybe, *Three Little Fishies* or *Harbor Lights*. I only see her in my mind, as we never had a picture taken, even at our wedding. She was always conscious of a tiny scar she had on her left cheek, or so she said, anyway it was never a big issue.

*   *   *

I went into selling real estate, wearing the grey flannel suit and conservative necktie. I am almost 6 ft. tall with brown eyes with thick brown hair, an all American Irishman my mother used to say. Every morning I picked up the paper from our front porch glancing at the headlines before I put it on the table. Invariably my wife would say.

"What's new in the world?" followed by " How would you like your eggs today honey?" I'd consistently reply,

"Nothing much new in the paper and I'll just take the eggs fried, same as usual." While she prepared the eggs I would read the sports page and as she poured the coffee she would say, "Watch out, it's hot."

So we started the day, read the paper, had our bacon and eggs followed by a quick kiss before I left for the office. Did I fail to mention that my shoes were always shined, a habit left over from the Marine days I guess.

It was about the second year into our marriage that things changed, slightly to be sure, but changed nevertheless. Now I have never written much about my wife because I really never knew much, only what little she volunteered from time to time. And she wasn't a great one for volunteering. She told me that she was an only child, born and raised here in California.

As I say, things were changing. One day when we were playing monopoly she looked up and said, "When I was a little girl my brother and I used to play monopoly and sometimes he would cheat and hit me if I told. I never really liked the game since."

Wait a minute—I thought you said you were an only child? But I let it pass as she went right on shaking her dice like she hadn't said anything at all out of place.

And another time when we were choosing drapes for our new home she mentioned some drapes she had in her house in New York. She looked at one of the material swatches and exclaimed,

"Oh this color is perfect the same green as the ones in New York."

"New York? I thought you always lived in California?" When I questioned her she seemed momentarily confused, then thought a moment before saying, "Oh I meant the drapes in my girlfriend Tina's house there."

I never asked about her parents, mainly because I did not want a reciprocal enquiry about mine. It would have been very hard to tell Doris Day that Rock Hudson's father had done time in prison for armed robbery. I must confess that I intimated they were both dead and hoped she would never ask to visit their graves. She said she had lost her parents too and that's all either of us ever spoke about the subject.

And then there was the subject of having children. I was making good money in real estate and would have liked to start a family, but whenever I brought the subject up, she came right out with, "I like it just being the two of us. Children are such a responsibility, you have to watch them all the time," followed by, "I love just being with you all by myself. We can wait a little while can't we?" And then she would change the subject. What could I say?

*   *   *

We were into our third year of marriage. Real estate was booming so we moved into an upscale neighborhood. We had a swimming pool and she bought a cocker spaniel dog. I put any thoughts about little things just not adding up on the back burner and by engaging in hard work, business ventures, and community activities, there was little time to be concerned about much else. My wife was the perfect housekeeper, cook and hostess and retained her beauty and charm. Our day-to-day living was ritualistically synchronized and at times becoming so predictable as to be mundane. This would soon change.

One day around noon I planned to mow the lawn when I looked out the window and saw two men leave their car and walk up our driveway.

When the doorbell rang I opened the door and was greeted by men both dressed in brown suits. One carried a brief case but the other, the tall one, was empty handed. I presumed they were of some religious persuasion that I was not—but before I could enquire, the short one opened his wallet and showed me a police-type identification.

"I am agent Jeffry Johnson from the FBI and this is Mr. Richter." I wonder if we might come inside and talk with you and your wife?" I examined his identification, ascertained it was genuine and let them in, my heart sinking as I wondered what my father had done this time but I hid this thought with a hearty handshake and called out into the kitchen as they were following me into the living room.

"Honey, there are a couple of men here to talk to us, could you come in for a moment?"

I could hear the radio playing and the water running and then both being turned off before she came through the swinging door wiping her hands on her apron. She looked almost frightened when I said they were from the FBI. Mr. Johnson introduced himself and then his companion said he would like to ask her a few questions.

She looked at me with a slight question in her eyes and one eyebrow went up ever so slightly as Agent Johnson introduced her to Mr. Richter, but her face showed no emotion. The agent was about 40 years old with thinning grayish hair and a round friendly face He could have been a Fuller Brush man intent on making a sale. Mr. Richter on the other hand looked maybe 30ish, but not at all well put together. His brown hair was greasy and needed cutting; his tie was crooked and he kept standing on one foot and then the other giving the picture of a tall lanky insecure young man. I have seen this type of Marine recruit many times, a man who needs polishing from head to toe. I made this quick assessment while my wife wiped her hands and nodded her head.

"I am Mrs. Amsbaugh, won't you sit down. Please excuse me for one second, I'll just let the dog out, he's in the kitchen, be right back."

The men took two chairs opposite the couch, and when she returned she sat on the couch next to me. We were facing the men across the coffee table. I hoped they wanted to buy a house but knew darned well that this was ridiculous. Agent Johnson opened with, "It has recently been brought to the agencies' attention that there may be some new information regarding two children found dead 6 years ago in New York. Their teacher is thought to be the last known person to see them alive." We both sat forward to ask almost simultaneously,

"But how can we be of any help?" Agent Johnson nodded his head.

"I am not sure. May I just ask you a couple of questions?"

"Of course."

When he asked permission to record the conversation we agreed and he opened his brief case, removed a small recorder put it on the table and continued by naming the school, date, and children.

"Mrs. Amsbaugh, we have reason to think you taught in this school, and he mentioned the school by name, have you ever lived in New York?" My wife looked genuinely mystified as she shrugged her shoulders then shook her head slowly

"No." After a small silence the agent continued,

"Do you know Mr. Richter? He says he is your brother."

She hesitated for only a moment before answering

"No I don't think I do." Then looking from Mr. Richter to my wife the agent continued.

"He says he is your brother. Is this true?"

I, I, I simply don't know!! I, I don't think so" She wiped her hands vigorously on her apron, appearing genuinely puzzled, as she put the apron down and looked over at Mr. Richter again. Actually as I looked closer at Mr. Richter he did look somewhat like her but there was not the slightest sign in her face that she knew him. However there was no time for me to mull this over before her alleged brother began to speak. When she heard his voice all expression left her face as if it had been cleaned with Windex. I felt almost sure she recognized him, and was frightened.

The next hour was filled with a mish mash of unbelievable data, allocations that completely changed everything on the menu of my marriage. My wife sat there dazed, as she continued to wipe her hands on her apron, now crumpled under the seemingly unending kneading. Perhaps I am getting ahead of myself. What followed was so amazing that I was, and am even now, unable to remember with accuracy the exact words, so best I just write the context as I can remember.

As Mr. Richter spoke she slumped back in her chair as if hit, then leaned forward and started to rise, but the agent put up his hand and stopped her.

"Please remain seated Mrs. Amsbaugh. I need to ask just a few more questions." So she sat back and her brother blew his nose, swallowed a sob before he quickly spoke,

"Our parents drowned a month ago in a boating accident. Up until then I didn't want to look for you Sis, as it was just too painful and I promised you..." He hesitated before leaning forward to mutter something I didn't understand and then raised his voice at least a decibel before continuing. "The truth is what is important now."

Little beads of sweat appeared on his forehead. He asked for a glass of water so the agent turned the tape recorder off while I went into the kitchen. I returned with the water and the recorder was turned back on and he stood up before continuing. "Our parents left a great deal of land and money to be divided between us and I feel it is my moral obligation to their memory that the truth be known."

He sat down obviously unstrung and looked down at his shoes, up at the ceiling and then out the window before he cleared his throat. "Sorry Sis, it was in the paper that you had moved to California. I didn't know what to do."

The agent rose from his chair. My wife put her hand over her mouth. Mr. Johnson spoke, "Please Mr. Richter I think this will be easier for everyone if I read the report."

When Mr. Richter was seated Mr. Johnson opened his brief case brought out some papers and paraphrased the following report from the New York Office.

It was in Upper state New York six years ago that two fifth-grade girls (and he gave their names) were reported missing after failing to arrive home from school. (He gave the date, month and year, and the name of the school.) "It was winter with blizzard conditions. The local authorities searched the area, but it was not until the following spring when the ice melted and with the guidance of a police dog that two small bodies were unearthed sharing a coffin under a single headstone Teater, across from the school. It was not until the coffin was opened that the police saw the recent occupants snuggled up to the original occupant. They were identified by dental records as those of the missing girls.

So, he continued, after a year the case was closed, unsolved until Mr. Richter came forth two weeks ago with this statement: "My sister was the girls' teacher. I saw her one day after school choking a child in the cloakroom when I opened the door."

As the agent read this, my wife's expression turned to one of disbelief. Her eyes opened wide in horror and her body tensed like that of a trapped animal. I was thunder struck.

Nobody in the room spoke for a moment or two. The cocker spaniel barked when the automatic sprinklers came on outside but the only noise in the room was the faint hum of the tape recorder as the agent continued reading. "It was in upper state New York six years ago to be sure but it was only assumed that the girls had met their death on the road home. It was a giant storm and others had been lost, so after the children were found there was nothing to suggest foul play. But I saw what really happened. My sister murdered them."

The agent looked closely at my wife before he read on. "She was scared when she saw me standing in the doorway watching her as she crouched down on the floor of the cloakroom strangling a child. Seems I'd surprised her and it was too damn late to stop her, as this child was drawing its' last breath, and the other was lying beside her quite dead. For the sake of our parents, especially Mom, who has a very week heart, I promised not to tell anyone if she would just say goodbye to Mom and Dad and leave the area. Signed JW Richter—May 15, 1952. The agent folded the report and put it back in his brief case. Mr. Richter looked back down at the floor then up at my wife. "I know I should have said something at the time Sis, but I was trying
to protect our mother." The room was as silent as an empty confessional.

After a few minutes of total silence Mr. Richter started talking so rapidly and in such an agitated voice that I wished for a button just to turn him off. The whole time my wife listened silently with her lips open in a sort of "O" position.

Then a small muted whimper came from her mouth as she looked at the agent and spoke in a pleading voice that came out in cry of disbelief, "My God !! That is positively not true. Oh my God."

She looked first at the agent, and then back at me. All the time clutching her apron and looking from one to the other protesting she honestly didn't recognized her brother when he first walked into the room but as soon as he started to speak she knew who he was and it was then and only at that very moment that the afternoon in the cloakroom 6 years ago came back to her.

Her voice gained strength and momentum as she spoke. I shall never forget her very words as she locked her eyes on the agents face. "Now I remember, I remember! How could I forget? My God, when I opened the door of that cloakroom I saw his hands around the neck of one of my children, and another little girl was stretched out on the floor next to her. When he turned and saw me, he said that if I ever breathed a word of this to anyone he would kill me. I asked him why he had done this and I honestly don't remember what he said, for I had to run to the bathroom to throw up. When I came back he demanded I leave town. That's all I remember."

She straightened up and looked directly at her brother for a few seconds before saying, "Of course Darrell, with me out of the picture, the entire inheritance will now be yours and who is to say what you told Mom and Dad. They are both dead."

I guess this was what she said but she was shaking and sobbing so much I couldn't understand anything more. She did manage to say, very plainly, at least twice, "How could you? How could you? Those poor little girls."

In the ensuing moment, the agent asked why she denied having a brother or ever living in New York, but before she could reply her brother began shouting so loud it drowned out anything she said. His eyes were glazed as he rambled on in a senseless way. Suddenly he grabbed the letter opener off the coffee table and leapt toward his sister. She dropped her apron and started to rise but as she stood her foot caught under the leg of the coffee table and she fell with an awful thud after hitting her head on the table corner.

As she lay motionless on the floor, a small trickle of blood drained from the wound in her temple. Her brother lunged for her crumpled body but the agent drew his gun and demanded he sit down.

It must have been the sight of the gun, for it was about this time that I made my really foolish move. Something in me just snapped and there I was right back in the Pacific in the thick of battle. I leaned over in the foxhole and heard myself shouting, "Stay down, protect your head and don't move." A Japanese soldier was coming in my direction with his bayonet drawn and a Japanese officer was right behind him with a gun in his hand. I had no choice but to kill them. Only I killed the soldier with the letter opener from the coffee table and the officer with my bare hands.

Standing at what I thought was Marine Headquarters my wits were coming back to me and I realized that I standing in the living room where there were no Japanese soldiers, but my brother-in-law and the agent both dead on the floor and my wife lifeless from a head wound slumped by the coffee table. I ran out the backdoor, up the hill and threw myself beneath the Sycamore tree. I sat there in a state of earthly purgatory before returning to the house to write this account. I will now call the police.

*   *   *

It was some months later after my psychiatrist at the Veterans Hospital helped me understand that my wife, perhaps honestly believed, that she had probably had neither parents nor brother and had always lived in California. She could have buried (he used the word repressed) any memory of her brother killing the children along with the memory of her family, where it remained tucked deep in her subconscious until she heard her brother's voice. This way she didn't have to grapple with the unbearable knowledge of what she had seen and the fear of her brother's threat. She also could have collaborated with her brother in the murder and simply escaped into a conscious or even unconscious role, the non-threatening role of suburban wife.

Then there is the possibility through greed for the family inheritance, each fabricated a story to eliminate the other. And without extensive psychoanalysis and more knowledge about their family dynamics it would be impossible to evaluate. The probability of an outsider, probably a psychopathic predator is another answer, but it will never be known.

At our next session the doctor said something like, "Now Captain, let's talk about you" So once again I put my head in my hands to ponder what's to become of me? Somehow I hope this may be all a dream and I will wake up to find everything normal. But then there is the probability that I am not dreaming and already awake and it is possible that I will wish I weren't.

Arlene's Answer

The year was 1933, five years into the biggest depression America would ever see. Banks were closing for lack of money and the jobless and hungry stood in lines on the streets for bowls of watery soup donated by charitable organizations, themselves running out of funds.

Looking around to make sure nobody was watching, she climbed up the ladder on the side of the wooden trash bin, and after putting one foot over the top, then the other, jumped down into a whirlpool of throwaways; old papers, magazines, bottles, broken dishes, boxes, bits of unwanted clothing and scraps of food all jumbled haphazardly together forming an enchanted forest. She marched slowly through the large receptacle lifting one foot then the other, her eyes wide with wonder. Along the far side of the bin she spied a small package, picking it up she unwrapped it to discover a bar of fragrant soap. The wrapper said Yardley's but she had not yet learned to read. After holding the creamy bar to her nose she put it in her pocket, climbed out of the bin and pulled it out periodically just to smell it on the short walk home. Her blue eyes, red curly hair and round freckled face made it obvious she was Irish. Her faded dress, frayed sweater and scuffed shoes laced with string made it obvious she was poor. Arlene O'Connor discovered the community trash container behind the fancy apartments when she was six. She then walked to her shanty in one of the poorest neighborhoods in New York City.

After telling her mother where she had been, Ma forbade her to go there again, but she went anyway. One time she found a chocolate bar and ate it all on the way home, the best way she could think of hiding it, but apparently not the surest as she threw up the sweet brown delicacy all over the floor an hour later. She told Ma it was dirt and then got switched for eating dirt. Ma, a short bosomy Irishwoman who seemed to get thinner after every pregnancy, was always meticulously neat. She put a clean apron over her dress every morning and kept her mousy hair neatly combed braided and pinned in a bun at the back of her neck. Her long fingers were capable of threading the finest needle or kneading bread with the punch of a prizefighter, or just gently rubbing the forehead of a feverish child. She wore no rings. A light sprinkling of freckles ran across her short nose and her cornflower blue eyes were framed by unusually dark lashes. When she smiled you knew her tea-stained teeth were her own.

Arlene's Pa, Danny O'Connor, at five feet ten was the perfect prototype of an Irishman. He carried an extra roll of flesh around his middle, had a full head of red hair, a freckled face, a pudgy nose and blue-green eyes that looked out under heavy bushy eyebrows. He often gave a hearty belly laugh to emphasize his words and had a unique way of rolling back on his heels when talking. Had he been a tad smaller he might have passed for a Leprechaun, but he had never found any gold at the end of his rainbow. He worked off and on in a steam engine repair shop. The fact that he had worked there for twelve years was no assurance he wouldn't be let go at any time. Something like twenty-five percent of people in America were unemployed and Danny's hours had been cut back to a frightening minimum.

After Franklin Roosevelt took over the reins of the country, Pa became optimistic with his talk of the "New Deal," a plan of distributing the wealth to reach the poorest of poor.

"You don't see any government men in soup lines now do you, Bridget? The government men have plenty to eat." Then Pa would say it again for if Pa said anything twice it turned into an irrefutable truth, the only requirement being for Ma to vigorously nod her head up and down and murmur in agreement. The NRA (National Recovery Act) gave him not only more hours, but also a slight increase in pay, which glued him to Roosevelt like a disciple.

Pa always eked by with a modicum of money to pay for his evenings at Clancy's bar, with always enough left to support his growing family's eating habit. Like Ma we nodded our heads as we finally saw more "chicken in every pot" (a political promise made by Herbert Hoover, the former president, although Pa always gave Roosevelt full credit).

The prerequisite for peace at the O'Connor dinner table was a bowed head during grace and vigorous nods of agreement with Pa's adulation of Franklyn Roosevelt.

It was only after this, the family ate.

*   *   *

She climbed over the top. The trash bin still fascinated her, if for nothing else than to just look inside all by herself to see what she could find. Arlene was the oldest of five sisters. Maybe she could find something for Molly the fifth O'Connor girl in line for hand-me-downs who had yet to wear a dress without a stain, mend, alteration or patch. Bridget might have even forgotten the time she forbade her daughter to go to the trash bin, especially when over the years Arlene had brought home beautiful or delicious cast offs in just the right size, shape or taste. Ma never asked where she got them. When Arlene was in the third grade she arrived home carrying a bag of apples and Ma made a luscious pie. Pa, not unlike Adam, just ate it, no questions asked. In fact, after finishing his first piece he smacked his lips and turned to Bridget, "Any more pie?"

Is it possible Adam requested a second apple in Gods first garden and Eve obliged? In America it looked like she may have done just that.

*   *   *

The O'Connor shanty always smelled like cabbage, Pa's cigars and the current new baby. It didn't look like Ma was going to stop with the baby thing until she had her even dozen.

It all stemmed back to the time Mrs. Houlahan's neighbor told Claire, Ma's neighbor, that Mrs. O'Malley had learned from

Mrs. O'Toole, who cleans the Cathedral, that by having at least twelve children, a mother could walk straight into heaven just like walking up the stairs to St Patrick's.

Once when Ma and Claire were hanging laundry over the alleyway between their windows Arlene overheard Ma say, "Four more babes and I will have earned me a place in Heaven."

After which Claire took the clothespin out of her mouth and called back, "Bridget you know you can count them three babies born dead."

Ma thought for a minute, then raised her hands over her head, "So, I'm headed to Paradise? I never noticed, Claire come right over for a cup of heavenly tea. Arlene brought home some crackers last evening." Bridget had her pride. She knew Arlene had gotten them from the trash bin but just couldn't announce it to Claire.

Over time, Ma and Pa would reach the dozen with a few to spare after adding four more girls then twin boys who always seemed to have runny noses, and a bow legged little sister with rickets, so bad a cat could walk through her legs without touching them. But for now Bridget and her neighbor had tea and crackers and dabbed the corners of their mouths with their napkins just like the real ladies in the movies.

*   *   *

On December 7th, 1941, a cold Sunday afternoon on the eastern coast of America, Arlene was standing by the kitchen sink peeling potatoes when she heard the radio announce that the Japanese had just bombed Pearl Harbor. Neither Arlene, Ma, Pa nor Claire knew where Pearl Harbor was located. Only Claire gave it a guess.

"Maybe out in the ocean where they grow pearls?"

Arlene wouldn't learn it was in Hawaii, a territory of the United States, until the next day when the whole class got its first geography lesson on the Pacific Islands.

Arlene was 14 when the Japanese bombed Pearl Harbor, starting a war in the Pacific and shortly thereafter Germany and

Italy declared war on the United States, from the other side of the world, putting America fighting on two fronts.

The slumping economy got a break, as America went to war across two oceans and civilians marched to work at the factories at home manufacturing the weaponry, uniforms, and accoutrements for their foreign destinations. Pa's shop got a contract from the government and his hours immediately increased. More jobs meant more money circulating, and prosperity started to raise its head and wag its tail over the land. The Great Depression would hopefully come to an end.

The whole country joined together in a concerted effort to win the war. Meat was rationed to assure there was enough for the armed forces. Patriotism showed itself in music and entertainment. Love Songs were tear, rendering as young couples danced to romantic ballads holding each other close, realizing that life could be prematurely terminated and each dance might be their last memory together. Mothers wept and fathers stood proud when they saw their sons in uniform. School children saved nickels and dimes to buy $25.00 war bonds for as little as $18.75.

Arlene politely declined when a boy named Sammy asked her to the senior ball. She told herself it was because she didn't have a dress to wear and Ma needed her help, but the true reason was she had never learned to dance. It didn't disappoint her too much to refuse, for she didn't like the way Sammy looked at her up and down and then when he called her little Orphan Annie doll that did it. She was always self-conscious of her looks, especially the plethora of red hair with its tendency to arrange itself independently atop her head in little Orphan Annie curls. In school, she participated in very few, extracurricular social activities. She didn't mind, as she was a good student and had discovered the public library, often bringing home poetry books and stories to read to the younger children; *Alice in Wonderland* and *Just So Stories* a few of their favorites. She discovered *Nancy Drew Mysteries* for herself and thought of all the clues she could put in a story about the Dumpster, maybe even a body. What a good book, *The Body on the floor of the Dumpster* just might make, but she never got around to writing it.

*   *   *

Five years later, Japan and Germany would surrender to America without armed conflict having ever reached the American continent. It was August of 1945 when jubilation ran rampant on the same streets of New York where lines of hungry people with empty soup bowls had once stood.

Arlene had graduated with honors the year before, having no idea the lasting effect the war in Europe would have on her own life.

After finishing high school in 1944 she worked weekends and evenings at the A&W restaurant. Walking behind the fancy upscale apartments on Rhonert Ave. (Pa called them the rich houses) she used a short cut by the new metal Dumpster, an upscale replacement for the old wooden trash bin, but she was usually too tired after working all day or it was too dark to stop.

Around Christmas, she made time to stop in the dumpster to find a large selection of everything from cosmetics to ready-to-wear, along with a delicatessen of delightful and assorted sugary morsels. Arlene pretending to be a rich woman shopping at Macy's looked through the plethora of disorganized merchandise without worry of cost. One time she found a pair of new shoes that really fit, and a purse only slightly used, to match. It was the same Christmas she came across an almost new wallet for Pa. When she opened it she found a five-dollar bill, a picture of a naked lady with breasts even larger than Ma's, and a little package of rubber balloons. Well Pa was too old to play with the balloons, and she knew better than to offer him the naked lady so she opted on the wallet with the fiver.

It became a great game these anticipative perusals through the throwaways. If you put your ear up against the bin you could hear her conversations inside.

"Welcome to Macy's. May I help you Miss O'Connor?" Then pitching her voice slightly lower she would answer in a condescending manner.

"Yes please. I will take this necktie, and that yellow scarf and this shirt. And this glass lampshade and this black wallet. And would you have them gift wrapped please. My chauffeur will pick them up at the store entrance." After continuing the conversation Arlene would revert to her saleslady voice.

"Thank you for shopping at Macy's, Miss O'Connor, do come back again soon." Smiling at the stained rusty inside wall of the trash bin she replied, "I certainly will. Merry Christmas to all."

*   *   *

It was the week after Christmas when this teenaged shopper arrived home in the late afternoon to find Ma all alone standing in the kitchen doorway sobbing as she stared at a whole pot of stew all over the floor. Clutching her stomach she looked at Arlene.

"What are we going to do for dinner?" Arlene, I'll have to sit down a minute, can you help me?"

"Sure Ma, what happened?"

"Jaysus, Joseph, Mary I dropped the stew me lady what does it look like?" Arlene threw her packages down on the worn leather chair and ran to her mother over nine months pregnant, now bending in pain. As Ma started to apologize for dropping the soup three of her children came in with Pa right behind them.

The next words were his. "Bridget what the hell." Pa never minced words and this was no exception, as he asked Arlene to get out while he got Ma upstairs, "and keep the children out of the way." Not so easy in a house their size, but Arlene rounded up those she could find and marched them next door to Claire's. Telling Claire what had happened Claire told them to stay at her place until she got back and went to help Bridget. That night by midnight there were two more O'Connor's, twin boys. Fortunately Claire had delivered babes in the old country and there were no complications so the newborns were fine. The children, warned not to wake their mother, crept back to their home. Arlene crawled in beside her sister, cuddling up to her body for warmth. With the house full of sleeping siblings, she muttered to no one in particular, " Twins, poor Ma." Then she thought of the surprise gift she had found for Ma in the dumpster. She would show it to her after she cleaned up the stew in the morning. Snuggling up to Fiona she immediately fell asleep.

The afternoon after Mike and Franklyn were born Arlene climbed the rickety stairs. Her parent's bedroom door was open and Ma invited her inside. Bridget was exceedingly pale and it seemed like she didn't want to talk, but she did turn her head when she saw all the presents.

"Here Ma, I found a tie for Pa and some shirts for the girls and something pretty for you. If you don't like it I can exchange it." She held up the lampshade.

"Ma there is some writing on it, the word Tiffany right down there in the corner. It's all glass and in perfect condition, I wonder what the word Tiffany means, sounds like the name of a cat?" Ma shrugged her shoulders and said,

"Probably some foreign country."

Bridget looked at the glass lampshade, a soft green with little purple and yellow grapes and a leaf decoration, but she wasn't too enthusiastic.

"Arlene, did you get the stew off the floor?"

"Before I came up, Ma"

"Thank you, dear. That is a lovely lampshade. But Arlene, I don't have a lamp it would fit and we have so many things, I really don't think we should keep it. And now with the twins." It was obvious this was not the time nor place for a lampshade discussion, so while Arlene was disappointed she said as casually as possible that she would take it back the very next day.

Ma sighed when Arlene left the room with the lampshade.

The next evening just when the sun was setting, Claire looked out her window and saw Arlene walking by with something loosely wrapped in newspaper but it was getting too dark to see what it was.

Reaching the dumpster, Arlene unwrapped her package and gave it a mighty toss over the top. After hearing the glass shatter as it hit the bottom she threw the crumpled newspapers over behind it. Dusting her hands together in a gesture of finality, she turned toward home. It was time for supper.

It wasn't until years later when she was at teachers college that she realized she had tossed an artifact worth a fortune into that Dumpster. This information came to light, so to speak, on a field trip to the Metropolitan Museum where the name Tiffany took her by complete surprise. But for now she was glad to get it off her hands and get home before dark.

*   *   *

In the winter of 1944 Arlene graduated from high school and went to work five days a week in an airplane factory assembling parts for fighter planes. It was the year before the war ended, the year before President Roosevelt died. Assigned to a corner of the factory designated for assembling radios she sat by a girl, Sandy Allen, just about her same age. Sandy would have a lasting influence on her future, but that first day she just seemed like a tall innocuous blond, not overly friendly but as Ma would probably say just a nice girl.

As the economy improved with the impetus of war, the meals improved in the shanty, and now with rationing the family had more meat than they had ever had. Pa got fatter and was heard occasionally to say in an almost inaudible undertone.

"Never you mind that Ireland never did declare war. That's the old country. We're in the new country. Thank God for President Roosevelt. He'll put this country up on its feet again." Arlene wondered if Pa would have been so ebullient had his draft age children been boys.

With Danny's weekly paychecks it had been difficult to feed so many children or stretch one more potato or lengthen one more chicken leg. Now with Arlene contributing financially, the food no longer had to stretch quite so far around the table. She found work, cleaning house on Saturdays for Mr. and Mrs. Saunders living in one of the apartments on Rhonert Avenue in front of the Dumpster.

One Saturday Mrs. Saunders asked Arlene to take a pile of magazines back to the Dumpster. As Arlene picked up the bundle she said, "You know Arleen, the dumpster is that big box behind the building. These are some old Life magazines we don't need any more. Just throw them over the top I think the junk men come next week."

As Arlene carried out the package of perhaps 20 magazines tied together with string, she noticed the magazine on the top had Franklin Roosevelt's picture on the cover. She dutifully threw them into the bin.

The next day despite the drizzle of rain she took a pair of scissors, climbed into the Dumpster cut the string and retrieved the magazine. She told Pa it was from Mrs. Sanders and he was so delighted he tacked Roosevelt's picture on the wall above his chair.

"Arlene, me girl, you thank Mrs. Sanders for me. My what a fine picture—and how thoughtful of her. She knows a great president when she sees one."

Hoping Pa would never meet the Sanders who were both avid Republicans she replied, "OK Pa, I'll tell her next week."

Ma peeked around the kitchen door looked at the Roosevelt looking down from the wall then shook her head, wiped her wet hands on her apron and retreated back to the kitchen.

*   *   *

In the airplane factory, Sandy Allen and Arlene O'Connor sat side-by-side assembling radios for fighter planes. They took coffee breaks, then lunch together and a friendship soon developed. Bridget would have been quite right. Sandy was a nice girl. Her parents had been killed in an automobile accident when she was 3 and her brother 7. Both children were raised in Pennsylvania by a very wealthy, albeit eccentric spinster aunt, who died when they were grown, leaving them both large trust funds but once again orphans. Sandy learned things were just the other way around for Arlene who had no money in the bank but a house filled with family. In their own way each felt sorry for the other.

One Monday morning, when Arlene sat down on the bench beside Sandy she saw Sandy had been crying. There was too much noise around to enquire so Arlene just gave her a friendly

110

pat and waited until they could go outside on their ten-minute break.

"Sandy, are you OK? What's the matter?" Sandy shook her head and Arlene waited for her to go on which she did after reaching for Arlene's hand.

"Arlene my brother in Germany has been shot. The army is discharging him and he's on his way home. He will be in the hospital here for a while, then he will come to live with me. He lost a leg and something about his... oh my God, Arleen—I think he's blind!! The Chaplin wrote, but oh there's the whistle. See you at lunch." She released her hold on Arlene's hand and Arlene put her arm around her shoulder as the two girls walked back into work.

*   *   *

Three weeks later James Allen was released from the army hospital in New York and Sandy quit working at the factory to be home with him. The day she left the airplane factory she gave Arlene her address and invited her over the following Sunday afternoon to meet her brother. Arlene looked at the address. It was 1212 Rhonert Avenue, Apt. 101. She caught her breath when she realized Sandy lived in the same apartment building almost next door to the old couple she cleaned for on Saturdays.

The following Sunday found Arlene preparing the twins for early Mass, cleaning the kitchen for Ma and preparing the stew, then quickly combing her own tangle of red curls before heading out for Rhonert Avenue. She almost forgot and took the shortcut to the Dumpster before realizing she had to go around the other way to reach the front of the apartments.

Finding the brass numbers 101 nailed on the front of a highly polished hard wood door she raised her knuckles to knock at the same time Sandy opened the door.

"Oh golly, you startled me Arlene I was just going down for yesterday's mail. Come on in and I'll get the mail later. "

"You startled me too Sandy, I was just about to knock." But before Sandy could say more, Arlene smiled and said, "Knock,

knock," and Sandy, picking up on the old cliché, answered, "Whose there?" To which Arlene replied, "Arlene."

To which Sandy asked, "Arlene who?"

"Ar lean on the doorbell if you give me time. Not too funny, but the best I could think of at the spur of the moment." Sandy laughed and the friends hugged each other in the doorway.

"Gosh it's so good to see you. You are so corny with a capital K, come on in and meet James." Arlene looked inside across an oriental carpet, hand carved koa wood furniture and up at some imperious looking people in ornate gold frames, looking down from the wall before her eyes fastened themselves on the window opposite the front door. The sun shone through a big picture window directly on a young man, a tartan wool blanket over his lap and dark glasses hiding his eyes. He had the same straight tawny hair, ivory complexion and features as his sister, but in a size larger. Arlene was sure his eyes were or had been blue. His shoulders were broad and his large hands lay folded on the blanket. He looked like an icon sitting on a throne, for even the metal of his wheel chair and a signet ring on his finger took on a silvery sparkle in the sunshine. This image only lasted for a moment before the man and sun both moved and the picture became secular in mood. When the girls reached the window and after Sandy introduced her brother she excused herself saying, "I'll just pick up the mail and make us a cup of tea. Be right back."

James turned his head to her and said, "Sit down please Arleen, you will have to find your own chair though, got to be one around here someplace. I can't see so well." Arlene found one, pulled it closer, sat down waiting a moment before she spoke

"I really miss your sister at work. I like her a lot," James turned his head toward the sound of her voice and smiled.

"So do I." Then silence ensued and both were relieved when Sandy returned with tea and cookies. The conversation began to flow easier as they exchanged pleasantries, enhanced with stories of their childhoods. James kept the lap robe on his lap when he told her about losing a leg just below the knee, and was optimistic about adjusting to the prosthesis. The afternoon went by almost too quickly and Arlene, realizing she should be home helping Ma, excused herself, but not without promising she would come again next weekend.

She found herself living for the weekends when she would visit Sandy's brother. James was now walking comfortably with his prosthesis and when the weather was nice they did just that. They never talked about his blindness but he would take her arm and she would guide him down the street watching for obstacles, skirting around people, children, dogs and pot holes. They went slowly and would sit on the park bench sharing lengthy conversations. Arlene had never been so happy. The first time he brought her hand to his lips and kissed her fingers she knew she loved him, and when their lips met, by the very window where she had first seen him, she knew for sure. James never spoke of marriage, but if he had she would have accepted in a second.

*   *   *

It was a crisp fall morning when Arlene took James to her home to meet her family, just before he planned to leave for New Jersey. As they walked up the rickety stairs to the front door the usual smell of cabbage greeted them, as did a fight between her brothers followed by child's shrill voice rising above the noises of the interior. "Oh no you don't, Greta. It's mine."

Then Ma's voice intervened, "That's enough out of you, me lady, " and quiet reigned as Arlene and James walked through the door. Pa came in almost directly behind them and once they were inside Arlene introduced them. Ma took off her apron and reached her hand out before remembering James couldn't see. But Arlene skillfully guided James hand to her mother's and they shook hands, after which Ma, somewhat embarrassed, invited him inside. Arlene led him to the sofa, while Pa was gesturing to the three smallest O' Connors to stand up so their guest could sit down. Then Ma after setting the table, called the family to dinner. After grace, James had one of the most interesting dinners of his life. Arlene watched him enjoy her family to its fullest. Well, not quite all the family's fullest as Bridget had cut back a little on the soup for herself and Pa. The children were oddly quiet as they watched this man wearing dark glasses spoon up his soup and declare it to be delicious. Five-year-old Laura looked at him for a long time before she asked,

"Are you like the Lone Ranger, do you wear dark glasses so we won't know who you are?" James immediately replied without a glitch in his voice, "Nope, I put these on when I need to think. And I think I am having a good time at your house. "

Pa got in the usual few good licks about Roosevelt and a few questions about Germany, but concentrated on telling him about Ireland, skipping the part about the Irish never joining the Allies in the war. Ma and the girls said very little. Ma even forgot he was blind a few times when she smiled in his direction.

They left early, so Arlene wouldn't need to walk back in the dark and the entire way along Rhonert Avenue James told her with real sincerity what a good time he had had.

"Honest, you are so lucky, Arlene. I always wanted a big family and I love the smell of your house. It's the smell of home cooking, real people and if I may say so, real love. Do you look like your mother or father?

"Well I have me fathers red hair and me mothers figure and seeing my father is roly-poly and my mother has sort of mousy hair, I am glad it's not the other way around."

James laughed before he said, "I know you have red hair, I can see just a tiny bit of color out of the corner of my left eye and it's beautiful." He reached out tousled her thick red curls and then kissed her right there on the street. His breath smelled like cabbage. It was on this walk home that he told her the story of the shrapnel that was embedded in both eyes and how inadequate he felt being so dependent on others. He couldn't come to grips with never being able to see anyone again. They had just passed the dumpster when Arlene told him she loved him, but he didn't say anything in reply.

*   *   *

The Government paid carte blanche for a guide dog for any serviceman blinded in the war with the ability to care for it.

James procured the necessary papers from the Veterans Hospital and three weeks later he found himself on a train leaving for Morristown, New Jersey, headquarters of Seeing Eye, Inc. He would learn how to work with his dog, a dog who had gone through three months of vigorous training to learn how to guide his master, in and about city streets, obey commands only when safe, watch traffic, cross streets safely and even walk around overhanging objects in his master's way. James would stay at the Seeing Eye housing in Morristown with his dog, both under the tutelage of a trainer for a month. His trainer was a twenty-five year-old girl named Shelly. His dog was a two year-old German Shepherd called Vincent. James was a quick and retentive learner, as was Vincent, and soon veteran and dog were headed home on the train just a day shy of a month.

As he was about to board the train he turned to Shelly, "Isn't it ironic, the damn Germans took my sight and now one of their dogs is making up for it."

"James, I am German. My last name is Schmidt, don't call us all 'damn Germans,' maybe 'damn war' would be better. My sister and brother-in-law were both killed in Dresden by a bomb dropped from an American plane." Then fearing she had said too much she put her hand on his shoulder, "I am truly sorry for sounding so angry but war brings out the worst in all of us. Let us pray this is the last one. James, good luck, you have done so well you should go home and marry that girl. The one you met though your sister. With Vincent you are now independent. The government will send you to college, pay for Braille lessons and tutors. Go for it." But the train was screeching to a stop and she never heard his answer.

*   *   *

Sandy and Arlene watched as a young man in dark glasses stepped off the train in New York, his hand grasping the U shaped harness around the body of a beautiful German Shepherd guiding him into the waiting room. The dog led him to an empty seat on a bench where he sat down at his feet. Sandy rushed to greet James—as did Arlene—both vying for his attention and talking at the same time.

On the bus ride home most people stepped out of the way. When one man stooped to pet the dog, James nicely explained that this dog was a guide dog, and when the dog was helping him find his way it is best not to pet him. The man withdrew his hand at once apologizing.

A voice came from across the aisle, obviously a child's voice, "Mom, is that man blind? Why does he gots that dog?"

"He is taking it for a walk, I think it knows the way home."

The answer sufficed at least in the immediate area and true to the mothers predictions they were soon home where James took off Vincent's harness and after showing him the backyard let him in the house. Sandy's current boyfriend came by and took her to the movies so Arlene, James and Vincent had the afternoon to themselves. As time went on Arlene would cook for James on the weekends and Sandy thoughtfully would spend her weekends with her boyfriend across the park.

Arlene lived for these weekends. Rain or shine those glorious hours in James arms would never be forgotten.

The first time they made love, James thought it best to shut the bedroom door and leave poor Vincent out in the hall. He might think James in trouble and try to save him, a rescue James didn't want made. The Guide Dog instructors never mentioned the proper protocol for this in Vermont.

The lovers synchronized their lovemaking like beautiful symphonic music; James strong dominant and knowledgeable, and Arlene submissive soft and abandoning all modesty. Soon each would know every nook and cranny of the other's body. Arlene eyes filled with tears the first time she saw his amputated stump and when he uncovered his milky blind eyes, blue but useless, it broke her heart. He was her first and only lover. She had no love left for any other man.

During the week James was learning Braille at the local Veterans Hall. Arlene continued working at the airplane factory, now seated next to a taciturn black woman about as friendly as a lion guarding her young. She seemed to be watching Arlene out

116

of the corner of her eye, but when Arlene ventured a word or two she just bent closer to her work like hadn't heard.

And so for three glorious months every weekend Arlene and James walked to the park holding hands, came home for coffee or wine and then made love in the bedroom at Rhonert Drive. James self-esteem was returning and he knew he loved Arlene. When he had gainful employment he would think of the next step but for now he would just concentrate on perfecting his Braille.

*   *   *

Christmas day 1945 dawned cold and frosty. It had snowed on Christmas Eve. The O'Connor shanty was drafty—the rags stuffed in the walls were soggy or partially frozen. Arlene had not visited the dumpster since James returned home from New Jersey. It was almost too difficult to climb into a cold metal bin this time of year but the real reason was she was afraid she might come across something from 101 Rhonert Ave.

James and Vincent paid a call at the O'Connor's Christmas afternoon and James gave Arlene a beautiful gold bracelet and she reciprocated with a record album of the Ink Spots, and a box of milk bones for Vincent.

It was still early when James excused himself, complaining of a headache and Arlene stayed at home to help Ma with Christmas dinner.

The following afternoon Arlene wrapped some turkey breast for James and walked briskly to 101 Rhonert Ave where she found James on the couch complaining of a headache, nausea and an inability to swallow. Placing her hand on his head she felt his high fever. He was unable to stand. She called the Veterans Hospital and soon found herself looking down at James on a gurney in the back of an ambulance speeding across town.

In the hospital blood tests confirmed James had contracted bulbar poliomyelitis. Polio was the crippling viral disease President Roosevelt had contracted leaving him unable to walk, and was near, if not, an epidemic in the United States. James was put into isolation and would be dead within the month. There was no way of saving him, for the Polio vaccine would not be developed until 6 years later.

Arlene shut her mind remembering the day the doctor left his room and told them he had choked to death, she only vaguely remembered walking out of the hospital. But the ensuing years in teachers college were a lifesaver for her broken heart. Not a cure, but a lifesaver.

* * *

Fifteen years later Arlene looked back to 1945, the year the Germans and then the Japanese surrendered, the end of a war that was supposed to end all wars, a year too many people close to her had died. Pa passed like an easy and rapid ride on an elevator—James climbed steps of pain to eternity and her little infant brother Daniel died silently before even tasting the fruits of life. Maybe there were different routes for people to travel to eternity. She thought about Ma and her twelve cathedral steps of children. Not that she believed a word of it, but she thought about it whenever she heard the song *Stairway to the Stars.*

Her little sister with rickets finished high school and the twins' noses had stopped running in the 6th grade. Arlene remembered how often Ma had hounded Pa to move to what she said was a better neighborhood.

He would patiently answer, on his way out the door to the pub, always saying almost the same words. "Bridget, I am thinking about it. I'll be back." Then one night leaving on this departing edict, Pa returned home from Clancy's Bar only to die in his sleep. Awakening the next morning, Ma closed his blue Irish eyes with her long capable fingers after whispering something for his ears alone to hear, before she went downstairs to her family. It was 1945, the same year almost to the month, that his beloved President Roosevelt passed away and a month before Bridget's last child Daniel would die in three months. Ma, exhausted already, did nothing but cry for the next two days, then got up on the third day as if nothing had happened, made a pot of tea and began to sweep the floor, at first slowly but soon with determination.

At Pa's viewing, Arlene overheard Claire say to Henrietta Myers, "Etta, he left her just when she needed him most, a widow with eleven children Poor Arlene, now that she is the oldest girl, her hands are even fuller.

The war was over when Shantytown was torn down, and with government subsidies and the little money she had saved over the last few years, Bridget was able to buy into the new project across town. Arlene moved right along with her, as Ma needed her help and Arlene needed her family. Never again did Arlene visit the dumpster and like a store gone out of business, it would become a part of her lost but not forgotten childhood.

*　　　　*　　　　*

But that was 15 years earlier. Now it was Christmas vacation and she was going over her Christmas card list in the upstairs bedroom. Ma was resting downstairs in bed. *The Twelve Days of Christmas* was playing quietly on the radio beside her. Arlene wondered, not for the first time, why things came in twelve's; disciples, eggs, even clocks had only 12 numbers on their faces, 12 inches in a foot, and last but not least Bridget's children. Cheaper by the dozen? No, she said to herself I don't think so. Looking up from her desk holding a pen poised over an open Christmas Card, her thoughts drifted to her class of little first graders learning to read. She loved teaching and never tired of reading to her own daughter. It hurt to think that Val was growing up and wouldn't be Peter Pan all of her life, but would leave her to fly out the window into a life of her own. Her pen fell from her hand, leaving a black spot on the Christmas card. The radio was still softly playing *The Twelve days of Christmas*. It took but a moment to look back at times that seemed to last forever as they were happening. After all the years packed together like sardines in the Shanty, her family was now dispersed, remaining crowed together in name only in her address book.

She picked up her little leather book and thumbed through the pages. She thought of Laura's crooked legs, little legs clanking on the steps as she went upstairs in the old shanty, but now hidden beneath the habit of a Carmelite Nun. Mike and Franklyn—now two fine tall Irish policemen, Ian—a fry cook, married with three children, Theresa in New Jersey—married to an electrician, and Molly—who seldom wrote her family, lived on a farm with a man in Ohio. Then there was Becky who had died of breast cancer six years ago. Ma never knew Becky had become a Mormon and had to wear some kind of shirt under her clothes. She told Arlene she was happy with her new religion because now she would just pass over a bridge and greet Jesus. Arlene wanted to say, "It sure beats having 12 children," but in deference to Ma, she said nothing. Sheila—a nurse, married a local podiatrist. Looking up from her list she heard her sister Fiona turn on the TV downstairs. Dear quiet Fiona was one stair step behind Sheila in age—still a spinster and helping with Ma. Realizing she had overlooked Jackson, she took a moment to look out the window. His address would never change—poor Jackson, a drug addict ending up in the penitentiary for life after fatally shooting a homeless vagrant. Ma believed it was an accident. Perhaps or perhaps not. She signed a card to him adding Ma's name to her own.

There was a knock on the door and looking up she saw a tall blond teenager, her blue eyes framed with unusually dark lashes, step into the room, it was Valerie her daughter born 15 years ago on Valentine's day. Was this child a step to her heaven or perhaps the stairs had been eliminated? She never asked Father Joyce, for church or no church, she knew God was love and love understands. As Val walked across the floor the overhead light picked up the highlights of red in her hair, but it was her sparkling light blue eyes that were outstanding. She turned them toward her mother and asked

"Ma what are you doing? May I go to the Rialto with Jim? Gone with the Wind is playing." Arlene, still immersed in her thoughts of childhood, nodded her head affirmatively as she thought. Yes, so it is my child, just gone like our yesterdays—with the wind.

Arlene and her daughter would kneel by the grave of a soldier in Arlington Cemetery at least once a year. Arlene always placed a red rose and a lock of red curly hair, a lock that would gradually turn to grey over the years, on James grave. Valerie would place a solitary yellow rose next to her mother's. One year Arlene laid a tiny branch of white dogwood flowers beside the rose and whispered to the wind these are for Vincent.

*   *   *

In teachers college Arlene had written an essay, a paper required for her certificate. The assignment was to describe her home life and its influence on her beliefs and decisions. Her brother Franklyn found it years after she died and published this one paragraph from her essay in the New York Telegraph:

Our tumbled down wooden three-bedroom shanty was just like the one next door, except Pa had added a bedroom next to the kitchen when our family ran out of sleeping space. The neighborhood was one of conjoined poverty. We never had a roof that didn't leak or a wall without a hole. We had a coal heater for the downstairs and a single galvanized tub for both laundry and bathing. Our water was heated on top of the coal stove. In winter when it rained, Ma put pots and pans on the floor to catch the drips. One of my little sisters suggested we get chalk and play connect the drops but decided it was more fun to jump up and down in the biggest bucket. We only had one faucet for fresh water and a toilet in back of the house. With a dozen children it was a popular spot. We had chamber pots for night. With four or five to a bed someone was always crawling over me to go to the potty. I didn't mind moving over, better than the alternative. Ma and Pa's bedroom was at the top of the nine stairs. We divided ourselves evenly between the three beds in the other two. In winter the wind whipped the cardboard siding and the old rags stuffed in the holes in the walls grew soggy doing their best to keep out the elements. In the summer, no longer needing to share body heat, we slept on rugs on the floor, we sloshed in our own perspiration. I grew up protecting and loving my sisters and brothers. We needed each other to coexist in the blatant poverty plus extreme weather changes in New York City.

Perhaps more people should grow up together in a Shanty to realize just how important they are to each other.

The Census Taker

Rip barked.

For ten years now I have been a widower, yet it still seems like only yesterday when Sgt. Kelly rang the doorbell in the late afternoon and broke the news that my wife Emily had been killed by a hit and run driver. Rip was a puppy and as we had no family and very few friends. I turned to Rip for solace. Over the years, Rip and I grew older but Emily would always remain the same. Time has a way of doing that to you after you die. I never had the heart to change a thing in Emily's upstairs sitting room. It remains to this day untouched.

When Rip barked I went to the front door and let him inside. Ripley is my 12-year-old Irish Wolfhound who in human years is around 80 and in real human years I'm right up there with him. Rip and I are similar; tall, thin, and grey haired. If Rip stood up on his hind legs he would stand over my head. Crispy white whiskers emerge from his muzzle and albeit shorter, a few straggly ones peek out from my ears and nostrils. The old wolfhound has more hair than I, but we are both long in tooth, hesitant in step, and on par with the number of sojourns to the restrooms of our choice. This would be the fourth time today I would go to the door in answer to his bark. The words of Ogden Nash, A door is what a dog is perpetually on the wrong side of, came to mind. With Rip back inside I nearly closed the door, before I noticed a young woman with a clipboard in her hands approaching me.

Rip pressed tightly against me, a soft growl emanating from his throat. When she reached the door I enquired,

"Hello Miss, May I ask your name and why you're here?"

"My name is Azrael. I am the census taker for the World Book. May I come in?" But, as she already had one foot over the threshold what could I say? We proceeded to the sofa where I invited her to sit next to me.

Rip laid down.

Azrael held her pen and lowered her eyes to the clipboard on her lap. After verifying my name, address, and birth date, my breathing started to slow down then shortly came to a halt. My head fell back on the couch just before she stood up to leave. Rip followed her to the door his tail between his legs. Leaning down she patted him and whispered in his ear

"Stay. I'll be back."

Then I realized Emily was standing beside me. She beckoned to me to follow her upstairs. As we started up the stairs Azrael, the angel of death, went in front of us to guide the way.

Rip barked.

100 State Street

I was walking along the sidewalk in front of my house pushing my doll carriage, heaped high with dolls, when a tall man with a brown bag slung over one shoulder, bent down over the dolls. Holding a threatening hand over the carriage he said in a gruff voice

"I'm going to get that doll."

As he extended his arm out over the carriage our big collie dog, Babs, ran off the front porch and let out a throaty growl before she bit the mailman in the hand. Nana rushed out of the house to my rescue. I was more amazed than frightened and remember little else than the blood dripping from the man's fingers onto my rubber doll. I was probably five years old and it wasn't until years later that Nana told me the rest of the story.

The young mailman apologized profusely, begging her not to report it to the Post Office, as he needed the job badly and felt very foolish and sorry when what he thought would be just a 'leetle' joke on the 'leetle' girl backfired. Nana imitated his Italian accent perfectly whenever she told the story, especially the part about him applauding her for training the dog to protect her leetle girl. She sent him on his way with a bandage on his hand and a reprimand he would not soon forget, leaving behind a blood stain on Betsy's little rubber arm that Nana got off with Clorox. Betsy never smelled the same.

My mother died when I was born so of course I don't remember her. Nana—we all called my grandmother Nana—told me my father disappeared sometime before that, but that was all she would say about him. This left me, Jenny, virtually an orphan when my maternal grandparents, Nana and Grandpa, brought me as an infant to live with them in their big house at 100 State Street, a quiet upper class residential street in Pasadena California. I learned in bits and pieces that a very rich man had built this house for his daughter and then she died, and my grandfather bought it for a bargain. The sum of five thousand dollars seems to stick in my mind. That was a great deal of money in those days.

I guess the house really was big, for it had three stories, five bedrooms, four bathrooms a large kitchen with two pantries and the living room and dining room each had beautiful stone fireplaces. The endearing feature to me was the smooth wooden banister hugging the stairway, ideal for sliding down, for with a good start you could slide from the second to the first floor in record time. On top of this, or literally below this, was a basement divided into three separate rooms one used for storage, things like suitcases and Grandpas old file boxes, and a smaller room with cobwebs on the ceiling and dust on the floor and little round holes in a cement wall for wine bottles, peeking out at you cork first from floor to ceiling. Nana said some of the dusty ones looked like they had been there before Noah. I never ventured very far into this room as I was afraid of spiders, and I wasn't sure who that man Noah was.

The main basement room was my stable for a life-sized rocking horse, Tony. I would rock rapidly on the cement floor, my tongue making the clicking sound of a gallop, to escape from the trolls living in the bottle and spider room. A flight of 14 stairs led to the kitchen above. Once Grandpa fell down the stairs and when Nana saw he wasn't hurt, her sympathy stopped right there on the top step when she stood in the open doorway and looked down.

"Now Fred, I told you not to carry all those suitcases." I remember Grandpa getting up and rubbing his backside before saying,

"Alma you were right." He was a very agreeable man.

Nana was a short little woman with chubby legs and arms, legs which she could move with great rapidity, and arms she would flail about in unspoken expletives. Her motto might have been, do it now and do it fast. She dressed in conservative cotton housedresses and always wore a hat when she went to the store. She had one narrow streak of pure white hair running over a head of long graying hair tightly braided and held in a bun with metal hairpins, long pins that never seemed to stick all the way into the bun. I always wanted to either pull them out or push them forward, but she never stopped long enough. My grandmother excelled in categorizing events in time zones of past, present and future. She would recite the family genealogy from the American Revolution to the present and then before she lost all of our attention she would continue straight into future forecasts for all of mankind. It was very time consuming.

Grandpa Fred sold real estate, and I seldom saw him not dressed in a suit and tie, his shoes shined to mirror perfection. He brought to mind the picture of Abraham Lincoln, that craggy face and long nose and full head of thick white wavy hair, which Nana said he had because he was Irish. His last name was Reedy. He was a man almost six feet tall with an obsequious manner that had, without doubt, come from years of spousal obedience. His grey eyes twinkled when he liked something and his overall expression was one of concern and kindness. I heard the lady next door say that he must be a saint. Looking back now I think he was just one of those men who needed and appreciated a strong decision maker at the helm. I usually tried to slip out of sight making myself scarce when Nana would speak to him beginning her sentence with, now I just want you to know, Fred.

I left 100 State Street when I was 14. Today I have mixed feelings about wanting to see it again as I fear it would be too changed. I loved that house exactly as it was when I was growing up. Most of the time I got more solace from curling up on the comfortable cushion in the window seat in the living room reading a book than I ever did from my family. My greatest source of comfort was reading.

*   *   *

One of my earliest memories a short time after the dog carriage caper was my bout with the whooping cough. This was before Charlotte moved into the house. I remember coughing so badly I would get up out of bed and run around the bed gasping for the next breath. One coughing episode coincided with one of the biggest earthquakes Southern California had ever experienced. The very first rolling shake happened when I was halfway around my bed. I came to a complete stop and stood watching my bed waltzing across the bedroom floor ahead of me. I cried, gasped, and coughed simultaneously as my bed left me!! I had never heard of an earthquake and remember being rigid with fright when I saw the floor actually move in little ripples. Nana came running into the room flailing her arms about, grabbing me to her chest and muttering something about the end of the world, and the inevitable loss of her Haviland China dishes. When the rolling stopped and the world didn't we turned around to see Grandpa calmly standing in the doorway.

"It's alright Alma, everything is just fine the world is not ending just rolling about a bit." Then he told me what an earthquake was and how California had quite a few, no need to worry. I felt better.

Nana calmed down and went downstairs to inspect her dishes now that she was convinced she might use them again.

When I heard Nana telling Grandpa about the world coming to an end it exacerbated my fear of going to bed at night upstairs. To reach my bedroom I had to walk down what seemed to me a long hallway, the whole way fearful that Jesus would appear and take us all up to heaven in some sort of cloud. Nana was banking on it, ever since our neighbor Mrs. Hinkley had taken her to a religious revival meeting somewhere in Hollywood. She learned there was something called Armageddon a terrible war that would end the world. Nana and Mrs. Hinkley felt the world was ready.

Nana often hummed the hymn, *We Shall Gather at the River*, as she cooked dinner, and nightly she turned on the radio to hear Amy Simple McPherson, a lady minister with a rasping voice preach fire and brimstone to the unbelievers. I was only five but Amy made a believer out of me. I remember to this day saying my prayers down on my knees before jumping into bed: long prayers of thankfulness for my blessings followed by petitions for the unfortunates of the world. According to Nana, who prayed faithfully with me, the starving children of Armenia were the currently needy.

During our nightly prayers Nana had the proclivity of talking to God like he was just one of the family reminding him of practically all the needs of the world mentioned on the KFI radio newscasts. Then we must mention the family needs and a nightly invocation to the angels to watch over various people all night long. I honestly do not remember this story but Grandpa tells of the time he was listening at my bedroom door when she asked the Guardian Angels to watch over Jenny all night long. He said I looked up in all innocence and said, "Nana forget the Guardian Angels, tonight I just want a little privacy."

Grandpa told me this story many years later and said even Nana laughed when she got out in the hall.

It was not long after the whooping cough and after Charlotte moved to 100 State Street that I added the Lindbergh baby to my prayer list. As a child of around six I didn't even know what kidnapping meant, but as Nana and Grandpa sat by the radio in the living room, listening to Edward R Murrow broadcasting the news it was apparent that it was not a good word, and that a very important child had been stolen. A man had climbed up a ladder and taken a little boy right out of his bedroom: a very important baby by the name of Lindbergh. His father flew airplanes over the ocean. Every night Nana and Grandpa sat in the living room glued to the news coming from a large radio standing in an ornate cabinet across the room from the window seat. Every day Mrs. Hinkley and Nana discussed the hopes of the baby being found alive. And when the child was found drowned in a nearby pond, Mrs. Hinkley gave a frightening speech about the devil in our kitchen followed by instructions on how to avoid being kidnapped. Nana was in total agreement. I was six years old but Nana and Mrs. Hinkley had a way of presenting rules that you would never forget. First you never talk to a strange man, second you never accept candy from a stranger and third you never get in a car with anyone that you don't know. I think it was sometime later that a fourth commandment was proclaimed by Nana. You never sit on a public toilet seat. I was never sure if Mrs. Hinkley was aware of this one.

*   *   *

Just after I was six, my life lost much of its tranquility when Cousin Charlotte, ten years older than I, joined us. Her yellow hair was braided in two pigtails. As a child looking into her face I never quite knew if I had pleased her or not, for one side of her mouth would twist down in a grimace while the other would turn up in a half smile. It seemed to be an expression she only saved for me, and when she started wearing lipstick it became even more menacing. However, the hostility in her eyes left little doubt. She disliked me. This would have been just fine if I didn't have to see her everyday but that was not to be for she was my cousin Charlotte, my grandmother's grandniece, Nana's deceased sister's grandchild, and she moved in with us. The year Charlotte was almost 16, her parents drowned while fishing off the shore of Nantucket and Nana offered to take care of her. She would live with us until she was grown and marriage took her off our hands.

Growing up I spent a great deal of time listening to others for very seldom did anyone direct a question or otherwise include me in a family conversation. Once when I asked Charlotte if she had known my parents she stood up and fled from the dinner table. Nana was always quick to come to Cousin Charlotte's aid and admonish me for asking questions so I seldom did. Often after dinner I would just take a book and head for the window seat. I knew the family history of *The Five Little Peppers and How They Grew*, one of my favorite books, much better than I did my own.

Years later I learned, from one of Nana's friends, that Charlotte was the product of a doting mother, a mother who spent her life running interference for anything and everything her daughter said or did. My cousin had been perfect in her mother's eyes, always first, best and the most beautiful and she was not about to give this up to anyone within shooting range. Well, to get back to the family dynamics on State Street. It is true that my grandmother loved and mothered me with care and concern, but also true I felt I could never live up to Charlotte's perfect image. I was a tall black-haired lanky girl with dark brown eyes, and skin just a tad darker than the rest in the family. Charlotte had blond hair, alabaster skin and light blue eyes, eyes that would turn green in certain instances. Like traffic lights, green gave her the right of way and early on I learned not to venture off the curb. She reminded me of the picture in a book by a man named Spyri of a young girl named Heidi living with her grandfather in the Swiss Alps. My grandmother must have had the same blond, but now of course mostly grey, hair like Heidi's. At 16 Charlotte was so pretty that the boys were beginning to hang around the house much to Nana's verbalized disapproval, but you could see inside she was proud of Charlotte's beauty and charm.

At the far end of the living room across from the window seat stood a grand piano with a silk-fringed shawl draped over it and resting on of this shawl stood a large picture of Nana and Grandpa when they were young. On the piano top just above the keys sat a Metronome, a small time-keeping device, about eight to ten inches tall in a pyramid shaped box with a little door that opened to a long slender rod that ticked back and forth like a windshield wiper. A little sliding metal weight could be moved up or down to regulate its speed. The further up on the rod you slid the weight, the slower the tick, and of course vice versa. I could play chopsticks with the weight at the very bottom, but only when nobody was home. I understood from Grandpa that the Metronome had been my mother's.

Charlotte could actually play tunes on the piano. I am sure this was subjective, but I felt she played with all the skill of an old maid piano teacher. Everything in perfect rhythm—ah 1, ah 2, ah 3—all timed by the monotonous clicking of that metronome.

There were times when I heard Charlotte and Nana talking and when they discovered I was around they would stop, mid-sentence, look sort of sideways at me and very obviously change the subject.

One day, when I was standing out of sight behind the kitchen door listening I heard Nana say, "I wish Jenny had our Nordic hair and the blue eyes, she looks so like her father. Immediately I looked up the word Nordic in the dictionary. Sure enough, it meant Scandinavian, tall, fair-haired and blue-eyed.

Aha! So that was the problem. My brown eyes and black hair just didn't do it. But my brown eyes could cry and they did so that day when I went into the living room and sequestered myself with a book in the corner of the window seat.

*   *   *

Charlotte and I went to different schools. Grandpa drove her to the local high school, but I could walk to my grammar school. I usually stopped to pick up Janet Durst at her home just about two blocks from the school and we would walk the rest of the way together. Janet had a black maid, Bella, who helped her get ready for school and would often be combing Janet's hair if I got to her house early. As there was no school cafeteria we had to take our lunches. Bella would always cut the crusts off Janet's sandwiches, a culinary art that escaped my grandmother completely as did the lengthwise cutting of the skin of an orange to make peeling easier. We each clutched a dime for a bottle of milk.

Sometimes, after school, we played at Janet's house. Her mother worked so we had the whole house to ourselves as Bella was almost always in the kitchen reading movie magazines. Janet's mother had the most beautiful bedroom, a big bed stacked high with satin pillows, a dressing table with bottles of perfume all shapes and sizes and a closet with silky sheer dressing gowns of all colors, my very favorites had fluffy white feathers down the front. But the piece de resistance for me were the beautiful shoes. All colors, high heels with jewel-like buckles. Alligators and snakes metamorphosed into pointed toes and spike heels sat side-by-side on the closet floor beside the most beautiful pair of golden embroidered Japanese slippers. Janet explained that her mother gave many parties. I had never seen Mrs. Durst but imagined that she must have looked and smelled wonderful. One afternoon Janet took me downstairs to the living room where she showed me a spot on the carpet in front of the liquor bar and made me promise not to say anything.

After crossing my heart and promising not to say a word, she whispered, "Last night my mother threw up all over the floor and Uncle Bernie carried her upstairs. She missed her whole party and so did Uncle Bernie. I think he stayed in her room to take care of her. I heard them laughing, so I guess she felt better by morning. He made me promise not to tell anyone because it would embarrass my mother too much. Bella cleaned up the carpet."

I felt so sorry for Mrs. Durst getting the flu like that. Then I asked Janet about her father.

"Oh, they are divorced. I think my father is in New York. He sends me money for my birthday."

I then told her in secret that I thought maybe my father was dead, as he never sent me anything but I didn't know. We parted that day with the sisterhood handshake of the first meeting of the SFS (Secret Father's Society) with a promise to always meet in secret on Father's Day. I don't think this society lasted a year, for Janet's mother married another man and a real father and step- father seemed too much for her to celebrate at the same time especially when Janet told me she didn't like her step-father.

Arroyo Seco School went through the 6th grade. By today's standards, it would have been small. I can remember all my teacher's names, and I am sure if they can't remember mine they most certainly can recall my Grandmother's. Nana marched me through the open houses like Sherman's march to the sea. I liked school and perhaps not having to compete with Charlotte was some help, as I seemed to do better with my own age group. We wore cotton dresses, the kind that had starched full skirts, white collars, puffed sleeves and sashes tied in a fluffy bow in the back. It was very popular to trade sashes for the day with your best girlfriend. I had two best friends, Joanne Chase and Marcia Holmes, besides Janet Durst who was my very best friend. Joanne used to cheat on tests but the worst thing Marcia ever did was throw up her breakfast of oatmeal all over the hallway one morning. It was a big breakfast and I thought for a moment I might just lose mine too. Then the bell rang and I chose instead to swallow quickly and run to my seat in Miss Perioth's 3rd grade class.

After school I usually walked straight home. I dreaded the walk home as there was one boy, Byron Erkenbrecker, who would follow me, hiding behind the big palm trees planted between the sidewalk and the road like he was a big game hunter, darting from one tree to the other until the opportunity arose to run out, lift up my skirt, and peek at my underpants. Not too many opportunities arose before I hit him over the head with my metal lunchbox hard enough to raise a good-sized lump on his head. After that he forsook the panty patrol and took a circuitous route home.

It was about a week later when I heard Nana telling Grandpa that she had talked to Mrs. Erkenbrecker who told her that she hoped she could get Byron through grammar school before he, and here she lowered her voice, so I missed the word, some girl. And then they both laughed so I guess it wasn't too serious.

*   *   *

My contemporaries on State Street were mostly boys, and we used to play hit the bat in the street in front of the house. You hit a softball, and whoever caught it would get to hit next. It was safe to play in the street in those days as there was very little, if any traffic. Grandpa had a Franklin car, which tooted a-hooga-a-hooga when he hit the horn, but other than his Franklin and the ice truck and a couple of cars belonging to the neighbors very few cars ever drove by.

The ice truck was a large covered truck carrying canvas-covered blocks of ice to replenish our icebox supply. Hanging by large hooks on the side of the truck were huge ice tongs and gigantic ropes used to carry the big blocks in the houses. The ice men were huge atlas types of men able to heave what looked like a square glacier over one shoulder and carry it into the house. Their hairy chests, armpits and bulging muscles were a source of wonder. Just watching them swing those big blocks into the ice compartment of our icebox in a single downswing was a phenomenal sight.

One day when I was around ten years old I ran across the street in front of the house and misjudging my distance ran too close behind the ice truck. I got safely to the middle of the street directly behind the truck when it slowed down causing the rope to swing out and hit me on the shoulder. I simply lost my footing and fell to the ground completely unhurt and certainly more embarrassed than anything. Nana, who had been watching out a window came screaming out of the house. The big burly driver stopped jumped out of the truck but by this time I was on my feet in time to hear Nana say she was going to faint as she fell to her knees. I ran in the house to bring her a glass of water and the big burly driver got an ice pick and put a little piece of ice in the glass. After telling us all, for by now there were quite a few neighbors at the scene, how frightened she was, and fanning herself with a piece of paper offered from the hand of one of the neighbors, the woman across the street patted her on the back and helped her into the house. The truck driver drove off and I remained standing on the front lawn, alone unhurt, unscathed and unsung. By the time Fred heard the story that evening at dinner the rope had narrowly missed hanging me, the driver was going way too fast and the side of the truck had pushed me down in the street. Plus Nana nearly had a heart attack. She did say the driver had been awfully nice and gave her ice for the water or she might have had that heart attack. For once Charlotte just listened.

I played with two other, girls my age in the nearby neighborhoods, and of course Jane Hinkley. It was Jane's mother who had told Nana about the end of the world. She also told Jane and I that if we went swimming in the fishpond in our lower garden moss would grow out of our ears. As we had already had a swim or two there we found ourselves peeking into each other's ears for quite a while. Then there was a neighborhood girl Denise Thumb, always pretending she was a boy, she even insisted on wearing boys' clothes. She wasn't much fun, maybe because we didn't like boys very much at that age. Her house was dark and dreary all full of massive dark furniture, and equally dark dreary servants. Grandpa told Nana that her father had invented sticky flypaper and he was worth a mint. Sticky flypaper was like two-sided adhesive tape, which could be hung from the ceiling and flying bugs simply stuck to its surface. The Thumbs moved away when I was in the fifth grade. I think Grandpa sold them a house in a very posh neighborhood on Orange Grove Avenue. I never saw Denise again, at least not looking like a girl. Someone told me years later that she had had a sex change and I wasn't surprised in the least. She probably changed her name to Denis.

*　　　*　　　*

My very best friend in the neighborhood was, of all people, the very old Reverent Haslett, an elderly retired Episcopal minister in his 80s who lived alone directly across the street. It was a steep climb up at least a dozen stirs to the cement walkway to his front door. He had great difficulty managing the stairs, as he was so short and stooped and bent almost double with arthritis and age. He had scaly brown crusty splotches like scabs on his head, which were just about my eye level when he bent over to walk. He had a Japanese housekeeper who I saw from time to time and it was rumored he had a niece but I never saw her. Walking with a halting gait, the grouchy man thumped his cane ahead of him each step he took as he grumbled to himself. The neighborhood children had branded him with the name grouchy man, the name would stick until he died.

When we went trick-or-treating on Halloween we used to ring his doorbell and run. That was before I got to know him. After I knew him I talked the tricksters out of going to his house. It was too hard for him to answer the front door and besides he never gave us candy anyway.

I would see him from time to time stumbling around his garden and for some reason I did not fear him. One time I waved at him and he waved back and smiled. Another time I climbed his front stairs and gave him a candy bar, which he accepted with graciousness. I did find it disturbing to stare at his scaly scalp and figured he just couldn't see it to wash it, and his nose wasn't up there so he couldn't smell it. Little by little we became friends and I would visit him in the afternoons and sit with him in his living room. He was lonely, and I suppose I was too, for we soon formed a fast friendship glued together by his National Geographic's and other pictorial magazines that we never had across the street. The Reverend was interested in the universe and the stars and I would sit transfixed as he explained everything from ancient Egypt to modern day astronomy. I remember looking through his National Geographic's with awe. True, I was somewhat embarrassed by the pictures of the naked African women, but figured the Reverent didn't know about such things, as he was too old.

One summer evening he hobbled across the street and asked Nana if I could have dinner with him the next night. She said something about that being very nice, for she was always in awe of men of God, so the next night I washed my hands and face, combed my hair put on my black patent leather shoes, the kind with a single strap across the instep fastened with a little pearl button, and climbed his steps to a lovely dinner of rice, chicken, green beans and salad served on his dining room table by his Japanese maid. There were even cloth napkins. Nana told me to remember that he would say grace so I dutifully bowed my head before dinner only to look across to see the Reverent had already begun eating.

He died when I was eleven years old, and he was ninety-four. We had been friends for five years but I knew nothing more about his life or his family than when I first talked with him. He did tell me it was his wife, when I saw a lady's picture in his living room, but never mentioned her again. He also told me he was from England. Two months after he was buried and his house had been sold his niece came to our front door, a short dark haired spinster type lady in a tweed suit and sensible lace up shoes. Introducing herself she handed me a brass candleholder saying, "Uncle Stephen would have liked you to have this." Then turning on her heels she left. After she left Nana shook her head, "Why only one candleholder? What a strange woman."

I had been surprised to know his name was Stephen but I cherished the candlestick. I never heard from Uncle Stephen's niece again.

I have a most vivid memory of one day in spring when the front doorbell rang. I was 13 years old and followed my grandmother to see who was at the door. It was always great fun to answer the doorbell. Most times it was a tramp offering to work for a little food. Times were hard and people were hungry. Nana would give them some chores in the yard and then feed them when they were finished. On this particular day she opened the door to an exceedingly tall man. His dark hair, tied with a thin leather strap hung down his back. That was all that I had a chance to see for when Nana opened the door, and before he could say a single word, she shut it in his face and pushed me behind her muttering, "That man is bad news."

After that strange things began to happen. One night all the electricity went out right in the middle of *Jack Benny*, Nana's favorite radio program, and didn't come on again until *One Man's Family*. Then about a week later we heard a terrible crash in the basement and discovered a broken window. About this same time Charlotte broke out in a mysterious rash that looked like poison oak. This rash did not help her image but it did my heart good to realize she was no longer so perfect and the rash was all through her golden hair. Toward the end of the following week Nana took my Grandfather aside into one of the pantries. When she looked at him and began with the customary, "Now I want you to know Fred," I fled. But before I could get out of earshot I heard her say, "Indians can call up evil spirits on the whole family. I remember in Iowa when the Indians came into Waterloo…"

I wish I'd stayed to listen for it might have helped later to explain a great deal. My grandmother was a great believer in evil spirits and the devil and although a Lutheran by trade (she used this expression herself) she consulted a spiritualist and doted on having her palm read as well as her tea leaves, and the spiritual discussions with Mrs. Hinkley could be the highlight of her day.

I continued to read and do my homework in the window seat. At twilight, a couple of weeks later I put down my *Nancy Drew* mystery story, *The Haunted Bridge,* and looked out the window.

What I saw was good enough for Carolyn Keen to incorporate into any of Nancy's adventures. The bushes parted and a man emerged from the underbrush with a knife in his hand. I recognized him as the man who had been at the door, the man with the long black hair tied back with a leather strap. In those days very few men wore their hair in that way, at least I had never seen one before. He looked right up at the window where I sat, but the sunlight shining on the glass obliterated his view of me and like the fictional girl detective I was emulating, I sat still and watched. I sat still because I was too scared to move. The man was crawling on all fours toward the backyard from bush to bush carrying the knife in his mouth like a dog would a bone. I was too caught up emulating Nancy Drew to let that one go, so I ran upstairs and looked out the back window, and sure enough there he was now standing upright under the apricot tree by the garage and staring straight up at our house. Soon he turned and edged his way to the back of the garage and fled. I was all excited with a wild desire to follow him and pictured myself jumping into Nancy's little yellow roadster, but of course that was impossible so I just watched from the window. By now I had developed a healthy imagination, nourished by the many books I had digested while sitting in the window seat. I was afraid Nana might get really mad or even tell Mrs. Hinkley we had evil spirits in the yard, so decided not to tell anyone what I had seen.

On a warm Southern California evening, a couple of weeks after I had witnessed the caper of the stranger in the backyard, I was sipping my daily Ovaltine drink on the front porch and waiting to listen to *The Adventures of Jack Armstrong*, the all-American boy, and *Little Orphan Annie* on the radio. I was working on decoding a message on the Little Orphan Annie decoder pin I had received for sending the station ten labels off the jars of Ovaltine, a chocolate vitamin powder added to milk. On the walk to the kitchen I decoded the message from numbers to letters and sure enough, the next day Sandy, the dog, would come up with a major find for Little Orphan Annie. After reaching the kitchen I found Nana peeling potatoes and patting a meatloaf into a rectangular shape to put in the oven. After putting the decoder safely in my pocket I looked in the icebox, but that wasn't very interesting so I opened the back door, peered outside and wondered what I wanted to do. The doorbell rang. Charlotte was in her room upstairs changing into her latest designer dress with matching high heels from Leeds Shoe store. Her fiancé, a blond banker of the perfect Nordic type, what else, was probably ringing the front doorbell, so rather than have to listen to all the greetings from Nana the, "come ins" and the "Charlotte will be down in a few moments etc. etc." I simply walked outside and found myself in the backyard standing under the Apricot tree. Something in the grass caught my eye so when I bent over to look closer, it turned out to be a single blue green feather resting on the ground. The feather, probably a turkey's, had strange green and white linear paintings on it, and it looked like the tip had been dipped in red paint of some kind. But stranger still was the tiny swatch of black hair resting beside it. I picked them up, held the black hair against my own hair and it matched. Putting the feather and the hair in my pocket along with my decoder pin, I remembered the tall man standing under this very Apricot tree. Perhaps he had dropped them. I knew that Nana didn't like the guy, whoever he was. She might make me throw the hair away along with the feather and somehow I just didn't want to, so I wouldn't tell her. I decided to put them both in my underwear drawer along with my decoder. My underwear drawer was so messy, nobody could find much of anything there.

*   *   *

It was a year later when I was 14 that this same man appeared at the door again and this time I answered it by myself, as I was home alone. Nana was at Charlotte's house, for Charlotte was now Mrs. Gregory, the result of a lavish wedding six months earlier. Nana spent so much time helping Mrs. Gregory at her house with just about everything, so I spent quite a few afternoons alone. I had somewhat outgrown the window seat, but still enjoyed the solitude of a good book, so when the doorbell rang I put the open book down on the sofa beside me. and sauntered to the door.

I couldn't have been more surprised. It was the tall man with his black hair bound back with a leather thong but now I saw that his eyes were almost as black as his hair. He was wearing khaki pants, a red plaid shirt and when I looked down at his feet he had on leather moccasins with some sort of beadwork across the front. His feet seemed small for a man of his height, not nearly as large as Grandpa Fred's. Then I looked up at his hands. On his left hand he wore a large turquoise and silver ring, and when his long sleeved shirt inched up above his wrist I saw a watch band set with turquoise. His fingers were long and thin. Before I could raise my eyes to his face he asked if my grandmother was home and when I said no he asked if he could come in as he had something he wanted to tell me. Well Nana wouldn't like that, and I was a little apprehensive too, so I suggested we sit on the swing on the front porch. Besides I had been warned never to talk to strange men.

Somehow this man didn't seem that strange, and anyway we were in full view of the neighbors next door so when he agreed, we sat on the porch swing. I was beginning to feel awkward but the motion of the swing was comforting as he started to talk. I just looked at his turquoise ring while he looked straight ahead, and began by asking me what I knew about my father. When I shook my head and shrugged my shoulders he turned and looked at me before continuing, "You may have guessed. Jenny, I am an Indian, an American Indian, and no, I am not your father. He was my twin brother. We grew up on a Reservation in Arizona and it was in what is now called Flagstaff that he met your mother and you are the result of their love."

I think he knew this was a bit startling, for I was only 14, so he hesitated and looked at me with compassion in his expressive eyes before continuing. I don't remember exactly what he said word for word but his revelation overwhelmed me. I kept looking at his hawk like nose and light brown skin, but it was his straight slick shiny black hair that was the most intriguing. It was so like my own that I wanted to reach out touch it, but of course I didn't.

He said my mother, Ellen, was a teacher at the reservation where she met my father. My grandmother was not happy, especially when she found Ellen was going to have me. I was so engrossed in the story I never ever thought to interrupt to ask if they were married and would have been too embarrassed to ask, even if I had thought of it. He hesitated and looked out from the swing to a child walking by across the street. In a minute, probably less, he went on and told me how my mother had died at the reservation hospital shortly after my birth and how his brother had told him that my grandmother, he called her Alma, swore to kill him, as the Indians had killed her Ellen, if she ever saw him again. Hearing this I steadied my feet on the floor and stopped the swing. I was so preoccupied with the fact that I was half Indian that I almost missed what came next, but his eyes held mine as he continued, in words that I remember almost exactly.

"Your grandparents came to the reservation right after your mother died and with the help of a lawyer gained custody of you and took you away to Pasadena with them. The white man's law is supreme so my brother knew from the beginning he must let you go. He also told me you would have a better education all around if you were with your white family, so Jenny, that is your story."

His hands were in his lap and I reached for them. Somehow, I wasn't frightened, but I must have sat there looking completely overwhelmed and all I could think of to say in a shaky voice that didn't even sound like mine was. "You are my uncle and I don't even know your name, or what happened to my father. Please tell me." I felt compelled to cover his hands with mine as he continued. I could see this whole thing was difficult for him and it must have taken a great deal of courage for him to continue.

"My name is Jeremy and your father was Tonka. Although always surefooted he somehow slipped over a cliff to his death right after you left with your grandparents." What Jeremy didn't tell me at that time was that he had his suspicions that perhaps Tonka had jumped to his death. When I started to cry he put his arms tenderly around me. I didn't know what to say, so I pushed the swing with one foot moving it back and forth as he put one arm around me. All I could think about was that my father was an Indian and that my father's name was Tonka.

142

"All your life I have watched you from time to time and saw that you were healthy and happy. I am getting older and you need to know. I must tell you now Little Feather, for your father called you that, that the hair I put in your backyard was your father's, it is meant to guard you." Hearing this I laid my head in his shoulder. The only sound was the squeaking springs of the swing as it swung rhythmically back and forth. By now the sun was setting. It didn't seem possible we had talked all afternoon. We were both tired and Jeremy was giving me a hug. I was wondering if I should take my father's hair and the feather out of my underwear drawer and return it to the backyard. But as things turned out I never did.

What neither of us noticed was that Nana, having come home, was peering out the window by the front door. Seeing Jeremy with his arms around me, she got Grandpa's gun from the front closet, opened the door and aimed it straight at the swing.

*   *   *

My grandparents grew up in the state of Iowa, in a little town called Waterloo, and were married when Alma was 18 and Fred 20. Iowa was mostly agricultural, with fields of tall corn for almost as far as you could see. Hot summer days and equally hot nights made it ideal for this annual cereal crop. There were frequent electrical storms and torrential downpours and it was during one of these storms with lightning flashing and thunder cracking that Alma had her first and only child on a small cot in the dining room. There was no doctor, as he couldn't get through the storm until the very last minute, so Alma delivered her ten-pound baby virtually without help. Her little girl, Ellen, was my mother. Alma vowed she would never have another child, and she didn't.

Waterloo was a small town with wooden sidewalks. A grocery and dry goods store and a furniture store with an undertaking parlor in the back made up the main street. Alma's father was the town undertaker. His name was Archibald McNeil Brinkerhoff, a name almost bigger than he was for he was, just a little over five and a half feet tall. He had a scar on his left cheek that ran from under his jaw about half way up his cheek, the result of a bullet wound received during the Civil War. He had fought for the North in Iowa's 3rd division and marched with General Sherman to the sea, razing through the South all the way down through Georgia. A more patriotic man you never would meet. He kept an American flag not only in the furniture part of the store but over the coffins in the back room.

After he came home from the war he married Mandana Olson, a delicate blue-eyed blond Swedish woman who bore him 4 children of which Alma was the eldest. She looked like her mother, but had the tenacity of her Dutch father. Mandana was a frail little lady, prone to asthma attacks and she had all she could do to take care of her 4 children. Alma was capable and a great help, so Mandana left most of the mothering as well as the cooking and household tasks to her oldest daughter.

Alma's father spend a great deal of time on the road, for it was the undertaker's job to pick up the bodies sometimes from distant farms and bring them back to the store to prepare for burial. He transported them by horse and wagon. A white horse pulled a small wagon for children and a black horse did the service for adults. In those days there were many babies that died and Alma used to cry for the mothers. She often peeked through the doorway when families would come in to pick out coffins. The poorest of poor families would have the plain pine boxes, without any linings and tops that simply nailed down in place. Her father mentioned that the poor Krause's from Des Moines seemed to be burying somebody in one of these, most of the time.

When Alma was about 12 she remembered her father telling the story of the time he rode out to the Kramers, a German family with a farm and more children than livestock, to pick up the mother who had died the day before. As the black horses stopped in front of the house, Rhineholdt Kramer, his overalls torn and suspenders drawn tight over an exceptionally dirty shirt, nodded his head as he stomped across the porch, muttering under his breath. When he looked at Archibald all he said was, "I can't believe it. She up and died on me right in the middle of berry picking season."

That evening after supper, Archie turned to Mandana, "It's about the first time I haven't felt sorry for the dead."

One time, Alma hid in a coffin when a man whom Pa called the stingiest man in Iowa, came to price coffins; another German from the Kramer neck of the woods, a Mr. Hans Strauble—he was always trying to get something for less money. Anyway Alma got in one of the coffins, shut the lid and waited for her father to step in front of the box. When he did she threw open the lid and said, "Boo!" hoping to frighten Herr Strauble, but all he said was, "I'll take that one, it's used." Then patting his big belly he belched before breaking into peals of laughter.

*　　　　*　　　　*

When Alma was born in 1879, Indians still roamed the streets of Waterloo, a scruffy bunch of unorganized Indians, probably Sioux, not the friendliest, but no longer on the warpath. However, they could throw a scare into the populace of a small town when they would band together, yelp profusely while jumping up and down and marching down the center of the street to enter the houses and help themselves to food or anything else that suited their fancy. They enjoyed these outings especially after drinking firewater. The residents of Waterloo soon learned to simply unlock their doors, so as not to have them broken down, and go into hiding until the inebriated Indians finished their shopping spree and left.

One afternoon Alma and her brother were playing outside when they saw a band of eight drunken Indians weaving down the street kicking up the dirt. Alma's ten-year-old brother thought he would tease Alma, so told her that the Injuns had come to get her little dog Tip, and would eat him. Before her brother could hold her back and stop her, she twisted out of his hands and darted out in the street, her bare feet kicking up the dust and ran up to confront the Indians. They looked into her wild frightened eyes, from their equally wild ones, not understanding a single word she was saying as she yelled and stamped her feet.

"You Can't have Tip You can't eat him," she screamed out, at least twice before one of the Indians grabbed her and lifted her, screaming and kicking, to the side of the road where she stood trembling until her brother ventured out from the back and dragged her to a wooden bench beside a tree where her little dog was tied. She grabbed Tip in her arms, held him tight against her body until the Indians had passed through the house, gutted the kitchen of edibles and made their way to the next house. It was the first and only time she saw Pa give her brother a licking.

It was shortly after this that her mother noticed a definite streak of white in her hair just over her left temple, a streak that remained with her all of her life, a streak she always tried to hide beneath her dark greying hair.

*   *   *

I do not know who now lives at 100 State Street. I would like to see it again, but only as I knew it growing up, and not on that terrible day when Nana opened the front door to her own death, for she collapsed senseless with a stroke as she pulled the trigger and shot a hole in the top of the swing. That was 10 years ago, but the picture of her falling there in the front doorway will remain engraved in my memory forever. Every so often in a dream, I see my uncle's face with a look of horror superimposed over a look of fear, as Nana fell in the doorway. I will cry out, and my husband will wake me gently, speaking comforting words to calm my distress.

After Nana died, Grandfather sold the house and moved in with Charlotte. I almost never see them, for I live far away in Arizona and teach school at an Indian reservation. My little twins Tony and Tonka exchange Christmas gifts with Charlotte's three children but other than that we pretty much go our own ways. A feather and a swatch of black hair remain tucked away in a little box, which I will always keep, of all places, in my underwear drawer. Tony practices the piano, often to the steady click of a metronome that once belonged to his grandmother.

A lone candlestick sits on the dining room table. I lost track of most of my childhood friends, but did read that Janet Durst married the grandson of a famous movie star and lives in Hollywood.

Miss Plimpton's Wheelchair

Her wheelchair came to a complete stop, just one foot from a drop straight down to a stony beachfront. No, it did not stop by itself, but was halted by the strong arms of William who had been chasing it as it gathered momentum down the 300 yards of grassy hillside. He grasped the handles but it was too late as Miss Plimpton had left her chair head first like a projectile straight over the cliff. Looking down to the beach and then up to sky he said, "Oh God, Miss P why you go there?"

He turned her chair around and pushed it back up the hill wondering why that old lady wanted to get to the beach in such a hurry. He secured the wheelchair facing the ocean on the covered lanai next to a chaise lounge. Nobody was in sight. It sure was fortunate he had looked up from setting the tables in time to see her rolling down the hill so he could put her chair back for her before lunch.

The lunch that day, in the Kalaheo dining room of the Halekapuka retirement home in Hawaii, consisted of tender white Mahi-mahi fish, yams and breadfruit with a sweet white wine sauce, and mixed vegetables followed by fresh guava sorbet and Kona coffee for desert. Too bad Miss Plimpton wasn't there as she liked Mahi-mahi. One of the nurses started calling her name over the loudspeaker right before lunch. Nobody had asked him where she was or he could have told them, but his business was only setting the tables, sweeping the floors on the lanai and lining up the wheelchairs so he knew better than to interfere.

At first he thought Miss Plimpton's wheel chair was running down the hill by itself. As a child he had not been allowed to speak unless spoken to and that was not often. He had been beaten severely for expressing opinions unless asked and soon learned to work in silence and his work at Halekapuka was just that; silently arranging the furniture, setting and clearing the tables, and lining up the wheel chairs on the back lanai. Only friendly nods and silent smiles to the old folks augmented these tasks. Anything more and he might lose his job.

*   *   *

The Halekapuka retirement home was on the lee side of the Island of Oahu. The Plumeria flowers on the trees gave forth a pungent sweet odor, the surf slapped against the shore and Hawaiian music could be heard in the dining room as William secured Miss Plimpton's wheel chair in its designated spot. Walking inside through the activity room he smoothed down his starched white uniform and looked at the two elderly people crouched over a card table. His business was only setting tables, arranging the furniture on the lanai and lining up wheelchairs so he knew not to interfere when the old man dropped a playing card on the floor in the game room. He simply left it there where the old man had put it.

*   *   *

Miss Naomi Nelson, a somewhat unattractive girl of about 20, was in charge at the front desk. There were 30 residents registered but only 29 to be found for lunch that day. Miss Plimpton at 88 was one of the oldest. She was missing. The rooms and the grounds had been searched but only her wheel chair was found on the veranda. She could not have walked the distance to the drop-off to the sea as she had two arthritic knees, which even on a good day could not carry her into the dining room. She never had visitors. She had no family in the area. Old Lady Plimpton had just dissolved.

Miss Nelson put a little check by her name and notified staff to start searching. The mystery was solved within the hour when Miss Plimpton was found on the beach dazed and shaking her head. A little girl had found her sitting up in the seaweed and went screaming for her mother.

"Mama, Mama, come quick! I found a witch on the beach."

Mama and child stood looking down at Miss Plimpton holding her head in her hands, her silver hair streaming around her face, with gentle frothy waves lapping over her legs. She just sat there dazed but alive. The mother took her daughter's hand and they ran home and called the police, who called the paramedics and the retirement home was immediately alerted, after which the old lady was rushed to the hospital.

Miss Nelson found it in her heart to visit Miss Plimpton in the hospital for the next two days, and found room enough left in her heart to slip a ring off Miss Plimpton's finger and slip it in her purse when the nurse was out of the room.

When Miss Plimpton had first arrived at The Halekapuka from Australia, she had told Miss Nelson all about the opal mine owned by her only living relative, her nephew. Miss Plimpton intimated that she was not fond of her nephew, so had left Australia and now simply loved living in Hawaii. Miss Plimpton was a great talker and everything she had said made it obvious to Miss Nelson that Miss Plimpton would not want this lovely piece of jewelry to go to her nephew, so who better to have it than herself. Miss Plimpton was somewhat confused and probably headed to the Memory Care side of the Halekapuka, so with this kind of reasoning the receptionist felt even more justified in helping herself to the ring with the big colored stone.

Within two days, Naomi Nelson had convinced herself that Miss Plimpton had given her the ring and each time she told someone this story it etched a deeper notch in her mind until it became her truth. Within no time she wore the ring with pride.

However, when Miss Plimpton had told the wily receptionist about most of her life in Australia, she had failed to mention a pertinent story that accompanied her opal ring.

The third day after Miss Plimpton's airborne journey to the beach, William noticed Miss Plimpton's ring on Miss Nelson's finger, when he went to the front desk to collect his paycheck. Miss Nelson showed it to him with great pride and he was surprised but guessed she didn't know the story that went with it. Oh well, it was none of his business. His business was setting up tables, arranging furniture and lining up the wheel chairs. He collected his paycheck in silence and went home.

The evening, before Miss Plimpton had chosen to dive onto the beach, he had overheard her at dinner talking about the opal ring she was wearing—some story about it being bad luck to wear an opal if it wasn't your birthstone. He was removing her empty soup bowl when he overheard her say, "The opal in this ring belonged to a great lady in Australia who died falling down a flight of stairs, and before that it had belonged to a lady who fell into an open mine shaft, and even before that another woman who had it committed suicide and then"... but he was through the swinging door and into the kitchen before her list was finished.

However he came back just in time to hear Miss Plimpton say none of the former owners had been born in October, for bad luck would befall anyone who wears an opal that was not born in that month. She ended her story with a little laugh and the words, "I was born October 22nd, too many years ago than I care to remember. And the opal is good luck for those of us born in October."

*   *   *

A week later the director of The Halekapuka got a phone call from Queens Hospital that Miss Naomi Nelson would not be in the next day. She was in intensive care and not expected to live and she didn't. The obituary in the Honolulu Advertiser next day reported that a Naomi Nelson, 20 years of age, born April 1,1984, on the big Island of Hawaii, had died of complications after falling from a horse. She is survived by her father and one brother.

Two weeks later, to the day, Miss Plimpton was back in the dining room, remarkably recovered. When William watched her pick up her dinner napkin he looked at her empty finger and thought to himself, Too bad the nice little receptionist die just after Miss Plimpton give her the ring. Oh well, it not my business

*   *   *

Late that afternoon William was arranging the wheelchairs on the lanai when he overheard a conversation between two visitors seated at a corner table; a young man who looked strangely familiar was talking to an older man. The young man lowered his voice. "I went through everything in Naomi's apartment after she died but found nothing there worth taking. I only have a ring I slipped off her finger before she died when she was unconscious in the hospital. Look!" he said, stretching his arm across the table and showed his companion his wristwatch. "I took out this colored stone from the ring and put it in my watchband so I can think of her back on the Big Island, after all she was my twin and I'll miss her."

Yes, William thought to himself just before he left to set the tables in the dining room, now I remember, he does look like Miss Nelson.

Phone Me

In the living room, on the couch, Amanda James uncurled her legs from beneath her and yawned in sheer boredom as she stretched her arms up over her head. Looking up at the wall clock she saw it was too early to think about making dinner, but too late to go shopping at the mall. Removing her glasses she put them down on the coffee room beside her magazine. Without a definite destination in mind she stood up and walked aimlessly through the kitchen, down the hall and into the bathroom where she stood for a moment and gazed at her image in the full-length mirror. Reaching for a comb beside the basin, her hand stopped in midair and she caught her breath when she heard the front door click open, followed by the creaking of the floorboards in the hallway. Her hand remained in midair as she told herself it was probably nothing, just time creeping up. But she knew full well time was soundless. Then she looked in the mirror.

The mirror over the basin was filled with the reflection of a man. Her hand fell to her side. She wanted to turn and run but her legs refused to cooperate. Transfixed, she stood motionless and stared. Somehow it registered to her that she knew him or had seen him before, but without her glasses she couldn't make out his features. Like two statues neither spoke. Then as surreptitiously as he had appeared he disappeared. The mirror once again reflected only the open doorway. Holding her breath she heard the front door click closed and after a few minutes of silence she ventured out into the hall. It had all happened so quickly that for a moment she thought it might have been her imagination.

After a thorough search of the house she was satisfied nothing was missing so she reasoned it useless to call the police as there was no sign of breaking or entering. It had been remiss of her to leave the door unlocked in the first place. She knew any woman living alone should keep her door locked, she had just forgotten. What would she tell the police? Would she tell them that a man had walked in just looked at her and left? Hardly!! She made herself a drink.

*   *   *

In November it had been six months, but it seemed like only yesterday, when she found her husband stretched out in bed, his lifeless eyes open, his body stiff and cold. The death certificate read death by natural causes.

Roger James would periodically stop breathing in his sleep, then catch his breath for a moment of silence followed by a frantic gasping for air before resuming his regular cadence of rolling snores. The doctor diagnosed it as sleep apnea and advised him to lose weight but he never did. In fact the apnea had begun when he started putting on weight and worsened, as he got heavier. At first it was frightening, then annoying, and finally just plain maddening. If he slept quietly for too long she found herself waking up just to wait for a strident air intake. She had tried sleeping in another bedroom but found she was straining to hear him, so moved back into her bed. Other than the glitches in his nighttime breathing Roger was perfect, for he gave her everything she wanted, perhaps to make up for his exasperating nocturnal disturbances.

Amanda, a tiny black haired lady from Irish-Italian heritage, had deep blue eyes, eyelashes she thickened with mascara and full red lips injected with collagen. This lent her face the flirtatious expression of a femme fatale, or so she thought. Years ago with the skill of a plastic surgeon her nose had been made smaller and straighter than her DNA had ordered, and only two years ago her face had been peeled as wrinkle free as Saran Wrap.

Roger James, tall, fat and handsome, had a full head of auburn hair, and intense blue eyes and the ability of putting people at ease with friendly chuckles and genuine concern. His obituary described him as one of the finest trial attorneys the state had ever seen, or words to that effect.

After thirty years of practicing law in San Francisco and making wise investments, Roger left Amanda with a more than an ample trust fund. She didn't realize it at first, but he also left her with a big empty space that needed regular replenishing; a space he had always kept filled to the brim with flattery, admiration and attention, the three things in the world she needed most, after the trust fund, of course. Looking back she had no idea she would miss him so much.

When they married she didn't want children and made sure she never had any. Ten years into the marriage she had opted for a tummy tuck followed by Barbie Doll-type augmentations, which had held up, so to speak, all these years. Her weekly facials, manicures and pedicures were a must. Her closet was packed with clothing, some never worn, for her hobby was self-indulgence, as it had been since she was old enough to dress herself. She met Roger twenty years earlier at the University of California where they sat next to each other in a German class. After Roger finished law school and passed the California State bar he became active in city and county politics and carried on a lucrative law practice.

He saw her as a billboard advertising his success. Although she never expressed it in so many words she looked at him as her horn of plenty. For Roger the challenge of practicing law and for Amanda the egocentric thrill of self-indulgence made each of them consider their marriage a success. When Roger died she immediately bought a plethora of designer widow's weeds and tipped her head with satisfaction at her bereaved reflection in Macy's store window

The month following Roger's death she sold their big house and moved into a small cottage where she had lived an uneventful life for the last seven months. After shopping one morning, she drove into the driveway, opened the garage with the automatic door opener, drove in and clicked the door closed.

The grating rumble of the opening and closing door never failed to remind her of Roger's sleep apnea. Gathering her packages she walked into her little cottage, greeted only by the hum of the refrigerator. Outside the November sky had darkened and it began to rain. The weather plus the silence added up to such loneliness, she would have even welcomed a spiel from a telemarketer, but the wall phone showed 0 messages.

Walking into the living room she plunked down on the couch, kicked off her shoes, put her feet up on the coffee table, her glasses on her nose and turned on the TV. Judge Judy just didn't do it so she read the Oprah magazine. Within half an hour the rain had abated. Going to the window she looked up at the sun peeking through the clouds, then lowered her eyes to the wet empty street. Nobody was in sight. It was like one of those science fiction movies where people just vanish from the earth. She recalled the old saying all dressed up and no place to go. Unconsciously she was clenching her fists. She was not ready to go 'no place' with what looked like 'nobody.'

Amanda often thought of calling somebody but she didn't have many close friends, (self- centered people usually don't) at least not the kind she could call at the last minute for a casual get together. Her few friends had been people affiliated with Roger's law practice, acquaintances from city or county political dinners. Even though they had lived in the same neighborhood for thirty years, they almost never fraternized with their neighbors. Looking back, it seemed Roger was always either at the office or away on business, but it wasn't the same for then she knew he would be coming back. Standing in the silent kitchen she could almost hear his voice.

"Keeps the wolf away from the door Amanda, got to go to the office. See you soon."

She thought about augmenting her black mourning garb with a bit of color. Then, as she looked at the clock remembering the mail should have been delivered, she put a jacket around her shoulders and walked outside. Reaching inside the mailbox she brought out an assortment of papers.

Back inside house, she threw the mail on the coffee table and after lighting a cozy fire in the fireplace she sat down on the couch, closed her eyes, and dozed off. After a little catnap she awoke in a more positive mood. In fact, she was glad that she had sold the big five-bedroom house in Happy Valley with such a beautiful but high maintenance garden. She had always known the house was much too large for the two of them. The first couple who looked at it bought it. They had five children. The mother was obviously breast-feeding as milk was leaking down the front of her blouse, which she consciously tried to cover with her sweater and Amanda pretended not to notice. Amanda pictured herself in her position with sagging breasts from nursing babies and running ragged doing housework. Finding the picture repugnant she was happy with the lack of the burden of motherhood.

* * *

Now, back to the present she got up from the couch went to the kitchen, made a mug of strong coffee and carried it to the living room to drink while going through her mail. There were the usual advertisements for new windows, grocery specials, a restaurant coupon for a second free meal, and then she saw it. Tucked among all this mishmash was a handwritten addressed envelope from Lone Tree Colorado. Now who did she know in Colorado? Of all things, the letter was addressed to Mrs. Mandy James. Nobody had called her Mandy for years. Ripping open the envelope she pulled out a handwritten note, a note that would change things forever.

Dear Mandy,

I hope this reaches you. I remember you so well when we were in school many years ago and I have been thinking about you wishing we could get reacquainted. I am recently widowed and my only son, Andy Jr. now is nearly 23 years old. He and I live together in Colorado. If you would like to talk to me, I will be happy. You can call me (609) 543-8765. I am so lonely these days and think of you so often. I read in the Colorado News that Roger had passed away so I send my deepest sympathy. My wife too died some months ago. I hope you remember me? I know it has been a long time.

With sincere longing to hear from you,
Andy York

10065 Longview Dr.
Lone Tree
Colorado 80148

*   *   *

Remember him!! She had kept his fraternity pin concealed in the corner of her jewelry box and his memory sequestered on the back burner of her mind, since college. Nostalgia began to simmer. Should she stir it or maybe just turn off the burner in her head? Somehow, her evening got a little brighter in the small house as she held the letter and felt the warm late afternoon sun shine on her back through the window. With the envelope in her hand she thought of Andy, tall handsome blond blue-eyed Andy. He had married her sorority sister June, and shortly after that she had married Roger and their lives had never crossed again. Now learning that Andy was a widower she felt a surge of girlish delight mingled with curiosity to see what he looked like today. She wondered if he had changed much. But first and foremost she wondered if he would notice any change in her, perhaps her nose? She waltzed down the hall to look in bathroom mirror where she brushed her hair the appropriate forty strokes, applied make up and changed to a colorful dress, before she addressed the empty room.

"What the Hell! I'll just write but ask him to call me."

She knew he had always loved her and without a doubt this was the reason he had written. Without a second thought she sent him her phone number.

The streetlights had just turned on as she sealed her letter, then got in the car and drove to the post office. The grating sound of the garage door as it was opening caused her to clutch the letter and drive even faster than she intended.

Andy phoned her as soon as he received her letter. They conversed with ease, recalling their old times together. Mandy was flattered and amazed that he remembered so much about college and her college years came back to life in her head as they talked. She learned he was a successful businessman, the owner of the Yorkshire Alarm Systems now installed in buildings all across the United States. Their conversations soon became a daily routine.

Wholeheartedly believing he had never stopped loving her, she was no longer lonely, especially since they had become telephone pals. He did not mention June nor did she speak of Roger.

*   *   *

In Colorado, Andy Jr. silently cursed the day his father learned of Mandy's widowhood and contacted her. When the two of them talked over the phone downstairs he would sit silently with his ear glued to the extension upstairs, one leg crossed over the other, the top leg kicking the air in an irritated cadence. He had never heard his old man joke with his mother in this way.

Andy Jr. was not happy. He had been so patient with his old man, just listening to him talk to Mandy for what seemed like months, although it had really been but a matter of weeks, with never a single word about Mama; had he forgotten the car crash that killed her eight months ago? That was not right, no not at all. He hung his head and muttered through clenched teeth

"Mandy, Mandy sugar candy—I'll fix your taffy good and dandy."

After all, his mother had been special. He thought of the time she helped him bury the neighbors' cat after he told her how it had accidentally drowned in their swimming pool, and Mama had always been on his side whenever the school principal called to report a mischief. The time the Rogers boy was found bruised from a beating he had given him behind the school and blamed him. When he assured Mama he had not done it, Mama had assured the principal Little Andy was sick and home with her all day. Just thinking about Mama made him stand up straighter.

No, Andy Jr. was not happy. He was tired of listening to these daily conversations between his father and that woman in California. He wondered what she was really like.

*   *   *

It was an exceptionally warm evening in Northern California, when around dusk the front doorbell rang. Mandy opened the door just a crack to see who was there, remembering to leave the chain on the door, aware that a woman living alone should be very careful who she lets in the house. She had had been lucky two days ago when that tall man left without harming her.

Peeking through the crack she said, "Hello, who's there!" and then almost couldn't believe her eyes.

The sun was setting behind him, its glare made it difficult to see but squinting her eyes for a better look she knew. Yes, it was Andy—Andy York with a bouquet of red roses. Unhooking the chain she opened the door and blinked into the setting sun. Inviting him inside she heard herself say, "How great you look Andy. You are still tall and handsome and those touches of grey in your hair give you such a distinguished look. This is really a surprise. I thought you were in Colorado. You look wonderful."

He bent and kissed her lightly on the forehead before saying, "Mandy, I thought I'd come to California and surprise you, so I made a reservation on a plane and here I am. It's sort of romantic at our age and as young Andy left Colorado for a week … Well, I just called American Airlines on a whim and here I am. At your service, Madam." He bowed low after handing her the roses. She just looked at him, speechless.

It crossed her mind that he used to give her yellow roses, but before she could give this a second thought he put his arms around her and told her red was for lost love, and that he had now found her. He was so tall and she so short she couldn't look directly into his eyes, but his firm warm body brought forth long forgotten feelings along with totally unexpected tears.

"Oh Andy, it is really you?" He laughed and assured her he was Andy and his next words brought more tears to her eyes.

"I would have known you anywhere, you haven't changed one bit. Maybe even a bit prettier is all." She believed him, never doubting that it was true.

"Time has been good to both us," she politely said, as she took his hand and guided him down the hall. She kept up a nervous chatter that matched the clatter of her tiny heels until they reached the living room and sat side by side on the sofa. Sliding closer to him she took a closer look. The chip in his front tooth had been repaired perfectly it was probably a cap. Turning away she looked through the pass-through into her kitchen before turning to ask

"Andy do you still drink beer or would you like a glass of wine or maybe a cup of coffee?" Andy thought it over and decided on coffee

"Mandy dear, I'll have coffee if you please. I am a little tired from the plane ride."

A warm spring breeze was gently blowing through the open window behind them. Excusing herself she retrieved the roses from the hall table where she had laid them and took them to the kitchen. He reached for a magazine.

"One minute Andy, I'll just make the coffee and put these roses in a vase, be right back." He only nodded his head as he continued reading the magazine.

In the kitchen while preparing the serving tray, she looked out at her guest through the pass-through. It seemed such a short time ago he had broken her heart with the announcement that June Forest was pregnant with his baby, yes! Her very own sorority sister, June! Not only that but that they would marry. Mandy tightened her fists and ran her hands down the front of her dress as she gazed at him through the kitchen pass through. A strange feeling flooded through her as she studied him and realized she had built something in her imagination that eluded reality. Any libidinal desire for the man sitting in her living room had changed to distain. How could she have thought she could ever exonerate him. She stood in the kitchen bristling with indignation as she stared at him, sitting on her couch thumbing through her magazine and looking as if nothing had ever happened in their past. Pitching her voice as pleasantly as she could, she called through the pass through, "Just a minute Andy, your drink is nearly ready."

Returning to the living room she placed the roses on the coffee table, mentioning their beautiful shade of dark red before she sat down out of the direct sunlight knowing the fast fading light of the dwindling day would give her a more youthful look. After placing the magazine back on the table Andy turned his full attention to her. Her earlier tears had caused Mandy's mascara to run and when wiping her eyes she had rubbed little circles of blue black around their orbits, reminding him of a raccoon. He looked up. A little raccoon with long fingernails wearing high heels had suddenly entered the room with a bouquet of red roses. He would never phone her again. His only desire was to leave as quickly as possible.

They sat together in an awkward silence for a moment before Andy put his hand over hers inching his way toward her. He was about ready to make some pretext to leave when she jumped up to say their coffee should be ready by now, so he leaned back into the sofa to wait.

Back in the kitchen she opened the cupboard above the sink and took down a small brown bottle sequestered behind a box of Oxy Clean, a small bottle of Monocaine Hydrochloride drops. She had brought it with her from her old house, her only thoughts of how peaceful Roger had looked after his convulsions stopped. When the coffee was ready she poured two cups but laced only one with the drops. Putting the cups on a silver tray she carried the tray into the living room and placed it on the table in front of the roses

It was now dark outside and a warm wind blew the curtains inward from the open window behind them as she tenderly handed Andy his cup. He helped himself to both cream and sugar. She drank hers black. Mandy quietly watched as Andy tipped the cup over his nose to drink the last drop. It must break his heart to love her so. Now as he should have done years ago, he was reaching out to her. But it was a desperate reach to offset a convulsion.

It was dark outside and Amanda failed to see the man with a knife slip through the window behind them. Within the next second she looked down at a knife rammed into her body just under her ribcage. Letting out a rasping gasp, she watched the blood rush from the wound into her lap, blood the color of the roses. Her hands became sticky as the warm blood pooled over them and her glazed eyes riveted on the redness around her. Andy slipped forward over the coffee table in a wrenching convulsion, leaving Amanda space to fall sideways on the couch.

His hands gripped the windowsill as the young man lowered himself to the ground and fled the scene. Since he did not believe in the next world, surely Mandy would not meet his mother to tell her what he had done. But if there were another world he knew that his mother would understand. The room was in darkness. An owl hooted in the distance. The curtains from the open window billowed inwards as a warm wind blew softly into the now silent room.

*   *   *

Three days later in Colorado Andy Jr. opened the door to a visit from the state police. Sgt. Collins showed him his badge, doffed his cap and extended his hand in sympathy as he informed young Andy of his father's death, enquiring if he, Andy Jr. had been acquainted with a women by the name of Amanda James.

Whatever

Dilly had rented a 9th floor apartment in Chicago six months ago after leaving her husband, a womanizer of the worst sort, deciding to make it on her own. At least that's the story she told her new acquaintances, and by now, although there was not a word of truth in it, Dilly believes it herself.

With short dark hair and eyes as black as coal, this tiny women uses neither makeup nor perfume. Now dressed in black pants suits and sneakers, it is time to go to work. It is midnight. She walks out the front door, shuts it silently behind her and walks down the hallway to the elevator.

There is no other way of putting it—she is a cat burglar.

With no fear of heights and small enough to squeeze through tiny spaces, she had worked with her older brother in New York since she was a child and now continues this art of illicit entry and egress here in Chicago. When her brother was killed in New York she moved to her present apartment where she has now lives, self-supporting, for over a year.

She considers herself a collector of small valuables that are not too heavy. She manages very well carrying them home without any outside help. Jewelry, coins, cash and carry by Dilly, no valuable too small could be written on her business card if she had need of one. But her business thrives without any advertisement and with a good fence in the city she has no worries. She works nights and sleeps days.

In the same building on the same floor, a man in his early 30s, more fat than muscle on his short squat body, rents the apartment directly across the hall. The name Ellis is written on a paper tacked above his doorknocker. Whenever he and Dilly pass in the hallway he nods briefly then shyly looks the other way before walking on.

Early some mornings they find themselves going up alone in the same elevator but they never speak. She holds a plastic shopping bag, with the logo of a local department store, in one hand and a small black purse in her other. He wears a coat, a muffler, and a cap with Chucky Cheese stamped across the visor and often fumbles with his car keys, suggesting he is in a rush to get wherever he is going.

*   *   *

With Dilly it is the little things that please her, small diamonds, little gemstones, rare coins, priceless artifacts, etc. and so it was with the cartouche. During one of her first burglaries in the Chicago area, after climbing up the side of a darkened house and squeezing through a small partially open window, she found herself standing on a soft oriental rug. She had done all her homework; cased the house the previous two nights, inspected the garage and found the Mercedes gone, even disabled the alarm system after learning from the gardener that the family would be out of town for the next two weeks.

Now upstairs in the dark of night, the beam of her small flashlight picks up a dresser across the room. Wearing rubber gloves and pulling out the top drawer she discovers, tucked in the folds of an old woolen scarf, a gold chain holding a small gold ornament. She is ecstatic as she lifts the necklace and clips it around her neck. A Cartouche, a small, maybe 2 by ¾ inch gold ornament with a snake and an Egyptian hieroglyphic embossed on its face. Had she been able to decipher the hieroglyphic she might have left the Cartouche exactly where she found it. But at that moment she found herself charmed by it.

After fastening it around her neck she had never once taken if off. It became a viable part of her demeanor and she in no way dreamed she would ever part with it. However, within just a few months she will become the victim and not the perpetrator of its theft.

It was early morning and Ellis was tired but still wound up as his night had taken more energy and much longer than expected. His last customer had refused to cooperate so he needed to take drastic measures before she was convinced he meant what he said and they got down to business. He usually, if not always, got his way in the long run but just in case there was difficulty he always carried a roll of masking tape in his back pocket.

Now waiting for the elevator to reach the 9th floor. Ellis watched Dilly as she bent over and picked up the shopping bag she had placed by her feet. A Cartouche on a gold chain fell forward from the neckline of her shirt. He stood stunned when he recognized the name of the Egyptian god of evil, darkness, and destruction marked on it. He knew he must have it. He had to control himself, as she tucked it back into her cleavage, not to lunge at the girl and grab it off of her right there on the spot.

Once back in his apartment across the hall from Dilly, the man called Ellis opened his door and doffed his cap to an empty room. Then, with his chucky cheese hat still on his head and having eaten two fried eggs for energy he was starting to feel restless. Sunlight had welcomed the day and it was time to follow through with his festering idea for a short visit across the hall. He was thankful for this opportunity so close to home so he could go without his overcoat and muffler. The cap had always seemed a good omen so he twisted it around on his head so the visor could be read from the back, a little trick he thought always brought him good luck. He ran his hand over the stubble on his chin. He would shave later. Leaving his apartment he took the four steps needed to cross the hall.

*   *   *

Answering her door, Dilly was surprised to see her neighbor, who had never acknowledged her in the hall with more than a nod in a curt greeting. He had never once spoken to her in the elevator. She asked if she could help him.

He answered in a heavy accent she couldn't place, "Are you alright?" She thought that was a funny thing to say but before she could reply he pulled out a gun and motioned her back into the room to the couch. Now seated and at gunpoint she realized this was not a social call and she began to sweat.

After the Chunky cheese man walked in and they were on the couch he moved close enough for her to smell his garlicky breath, just before he reached down in the neck of her shirt with his free hand, grabbed the Cartouche and with two strong yanks broke the chain. The necklace became his. A look of fright turning to terror shown in the girl's black eyes and the smell of fear emanated from her every pore, the smell arousing a desire in his loins that took complete control of him. It became as clear as the sunrise outside that he must have this woman as well as the necklace. The moon was down, the sun was up and it was mid-morning when the two neighbors parted.

Another wife was acceptable in the land, where he had proposed to take her to live a life of luxury and she licked her lips as he promised her the Cartouche, if she would marry him and move to Ethiopia. He parted with the Cartouche in his hand with the promise to give it back when they were married. They agreed to meet in his apartment the next night. Had he turned he would have seen her surreptitious smile.

*   *   *

A week later, on the 9th floor of an apartment in Chicago, behind a door with Ellis written on a piece of paper above the knocker, the police removed the body of a man found stabbed to death. When the corpse was loaded on a gurney and wheeled into the hall, the Police Sergeant knocked on Dilly's door to see if she could identify it. After the Sergeant folded the sheet back Dilly shook her head from side to side and said she didn't know him, but had seen him a once or twice in the hallway. Answering a few more standard questions and watching the policeman fold the sheet back over the lifeless face of her neighbor, she stood in her doorway rubbing her fingers over a gold medallion hanging from a chain around her neck. The young cop was very nice and looked over at her, just before he wheeled Ellis to the elevator, to compliment her on her pretty necklace. She simply smiled and said, "Thank You."

The Enchantment

Day One

M y magic story begins with a rickety old car clanking up a winding mountain road. Bent over the wheel is a fifty-year-old man who appears twice that age with his wrinkles, runny nose and toothless mouth. An eight-year-old boy in the back seat is tapping him on the shoulder with an empty thermos but the man only shrugs, refusing to acknowledge him.

"Knock it off Philip. I'll stop at the next stream. Now just knock it off." No sooner had he spoken than the car gave a sudden jerk as a tire blew, causing the man to curse profusely as they vibrated to a standstill. After changing the tire he opened the back door, grabbed the lad and threw him out over the soft grassy embankment. The boy rolled down the hillside and came to a stop curled in a little ball, his head in his hands, alert but fearful of moving, until he could no longer hear the car shuddering up the road.

It was mid-morning when this small boy found himself in Northern California, in a forest of conifers in the mountains about 18 miles above the town of Orville. Cautiously, having crawled then walked, the boy made his way through the silent woodland, looking back over his shoulder from time to time to make sure he wasn't being followed. Midst the pines, stood a singular Madrone, a tree with reddish bark and shiny green leaves, and it was under this tree the boy chose to pause and look around. The ground was still damp from the rain the night before, but now the sun was out. It was early afternoon and he was hungry. He had one stick of chewing gum, which he folded and chewed, but he was still hungry. A squirrel chattered from a pine tree before it scampered away and a goose honked twice in the distance, before quiet again prevailed. Philip had never been in a forest before. His yard at home had two sycamore trees and a telephone pole. He forgot and swallowed the gum thinking his mother would not be pleased, as just for a moment he had forgotten where she was.

*   *   *

That same afternoon Janet and Roger Croft drove 18 miles up the highway past Orville and turned into a small gated community of cabins around Lake Madrone, a small manmade lake built from a tributary of the Feather River. The sunlight sparkled on the small lake in front of the cabin. Squirrels chattered in the pine trees, three melodious frogs sang in the little pond in their front yard. Roger stopped the car and they stepped out, unlocked their back door and walked across the living room, onto the front porch, where they stood looking out across the quiet lake. Janet, tending to be on the dramatic side, emoted with happiness as she stood beside her husband.

"Oh Roger, I am so happy here, I just want to stretch my arms around the cabin, smell the woods and listen to the symphony of nature. But I'll put my arms around you instead, as you complete my picture of paradise." Roger a tall serious pragmatic type of young man looked down at his tiny blond wife, the joy of his life, and took her in his arms.

"I'll double that babe, you said it all." They stood in silence for a moment before walking back through the house to their car to bring their suitcases inside. It would soon be dark. Roger made them each a martini while Janet opened a package of potato chips and turned music on the radio. After settling on the pink couch in the living room they toasted 15 years of a perfect marriage. They had met in grammar school, and were now both teachers. A lone goose out on the lake honked twice at the same time they raised their glasses.

Janet looked up toward the loft before turning back to her husband.

"Oh, that reminds me. I called old Elmer yesterday and he will be coming tomorrow morning to fix that cracked window over our bed.

*   *   *

Elmer and Betty were in their car returning home from the Indian Casino in Orville. The sun was setting. Elmer drove and Betty snored, her head falling back on the seat and her mouth hanging open, a little rivulet of saliva making its way out over her chin. Elmer looked over at his third wife. She had been a reasonably pretty woman six years ago, when they had married. He had just found salvation as a born again Christian and Betty had promised to stop drinking and go to church. During the past six years she had done neither. Even though she was 20 years younger than Elmer it seemed hardly believable what time and liquor had done to her. Her mousey hair was unkempt, her clothing spotted with food and the top button on her blouse hung by a thread. Gasping and puffing through an open mouth she emitted fluctuating snores upward as Elmer drove. His hands gripped the steering wheel as he sent his silent prayers for her salvation up in the same direction.

When they reached home he carried her into the house. Looking at her utter slovenliness, he couldn't help but wonder why she couldn't just die like his first two wives but understood it was up to Jesus; so placed her on the bed and prepared his own dinner. He was lonely. When a goose honked twice over at Lake Madrone it reminded him he must get his tools out for the window repair at the Croft's cabin the next morning. Elmer had worked over fifty years in the area and had a reputation as a fine carpenter. He had built or repaired most of the cabins in the Lake Madrone community just five minutes away.

*   *   *

As Philip stood up under the Madrone tree, he heard a goose honk from somewhere across the highway. Then he spied a trail and following it, for what seemed like an eternity, it ended and

175

he saw the car. It was twilight but he would have recognized that car anywhere. He fell to the ground in fear as he stood motionless in the underbrush, watching the man get out of his mother's old clunker, unzip his pants, urinate, then zip up his pants and step back into the car and drive away. Not far away, from a different vantage point behind a tree, a young woman also watched until the old car clanked its way back to the highway.

Terrorized, the boy cowered in the weeds until he heard a voice, a girl's voice, and raising his head he saw a tall young woman in blue jeans. Her hair was tied back under a red bandana and she looked down at him out of the bluest eyes he had ever seen.

"So, young man what is your name?" He sat up circling his right palm over his mouth and shaking his head from side to side as he mouthed the word no.

The girl soon understood and when it was substantiated that he could hear but not speak and he was hungry, she took his skinny little hand in hers and led him a little further up a path to her home. She cooked potatoes and gave him some cold chicken and a glass of milk. It took a great deal of time and many questions before Philip told her the whole story.

Astrid was the girl's name, and she did outside maintenance work for a small-gated community just a half-mile across the highway. She told him she was 30 years old, lived alone, and was from Denmark, He had never heard of that place but decided he liked her anyway. Light brown hair peeked from under the bandana and her blue eyes exuded friendliness when she smiled. He wanted to gesture that she was pretty but it embarrassed him.

She was having a hard time thinking where to take him, so when he asked to stay the night she made him a cozy place on the couch before she invited him to take a warm bath, fearful to ask when he had had his last one. She glimpsed welts on his emaciated body when she brought him a bath towel. She wondered just what to do about the man in the car. Philip did not know the man's name and gestured that he had only met him about a week ago. According to the boy's frantic hand motions, the man shot his mother, then buried her in the backyard before he forced Philip into his mother's car and drove away with him.

With this information from her houseguest, Astrid locked the doors and windows and decided tomorrow she would call her friend in Oroville who worked in the District Attorney's office. She would know what to do

Philip was sound asleep on the couch before the sun went down and when a goose out on Lake Madrone honked twice Astrid was loading her revolver.

About 9 o'clock that night she recognized the sound of the old rattletrap before it came to a stop in the clearing. There followed a rap on the door. Opening the door a crack, her right hand holding the gun out of sight, she saw the grubby old man standing in the moonlight. He enquired about a little boy.

"No I have not seen him." She gripped the gun tighter.

The man said he was the kid's father but didn't push the issue, then left. Astrid locked the front door before she put the gun back under her pillow. Philip had slept through the whole thing. Astrid did not sleep the rest of the night.

Day Two

The following morning found Janet and Roger in bed in the loft, the sun shining through the skylight, refracting through the glass crystals hanging from the ceiling. What a wonderful sight so early in the day. They both decided they could stay there forever, however maybe forever would be less enchanting, so they got out of bed and were finishing breakfast just as Elmer knocked on their back door. His first words were,

"Hey, did you know you all got a big goose in your front yard? It went yonder round to the side of the house when I came in."

Janet went outside to look, as she had never seen a goose up close and found it practically at her feet. It was bigger and whiter than she expected and as they stood looking at each other, the goose touched his beak three times to the ground before spreading his wings and with a swooshing sound flew off over the house. She looked down where the goose had been standing and discovered something that was sparkling. Walking over she picked up a large white feather. The feather was still warm. She

177

walked in the house and put it on the table beside the toolbox just before Elmer packed his tools to leave. After Roger paid him he closed the box, got in his car and waved good-bye. The new window looked wonderful, and Roger heard himself saying, "Hurry up Jan, we'll hike up to that big rock before lunch." Roger was very athletic.

When they returned, there was a battered old white car parked in the driveway and a disheveled man stood knocking on their backdoor, inquiring if they had seen a little boy in the area, as his son was lost. They assured him they hadn't and after he left Janet turned to Roger.

"We should have asked him his name or the child's name? He sure smelled bad."

You're right he did smell awful." Rodger replied pinching his nostrils together with a look of revulsion.

Janet had completely forgotten the feather, for she had found a beautiful pink rock on their morning hike. It would almost match their couch.

*   *   *

When Elmer arrived home for lunch, Betty met him at the door. When he opened his toolbox on the kitchen table, a large white feather fell to the floor. Betty was reasonably sober and expressed such delight that he said, "Here take it. It's yours. I probably picked it up with my things at the Crofts."

She tucked it in her cleavage, in close proximity to her heart and remarked on how warm it was. Elmer left on another job that would take all afternoon.

It was almost dark when he returned home that evening and Betty met him at the door. Her hair was combed, she wore an apron and the table was set. She was still a bit shaken from all the work she had done but soon there was a pot roast and potatoes on their plates for dinner. Elmer could not believe his eyes. At the table she bowed her head and waited for him to say the blessing. The tip of the feather, still snuggled in Betty's cleavage, peeked out over her apron. She couldn't explain it and

Elmer couldn't believe it, but on a wing and a prayer their life seemed to have changed.

Day Three

Mid-morning Betty went to the local general store and bought material for a dress for herself and yarn to knit a sweater for Elmer and her hands were full of these bundles as she left and literally bumped into the Danish gardening lady, which caused her to accidentally drop one of her packages. Astrid hardly knew what to think when she saw the change in Betty. She was sober and reasonable clean and tidy. A few minutes after Betty left, Astrid spied a feather on the floor, and bending down she picked up of all things a goose feather! She put it in her purse, intending to take it home to Philip, a wonderful thing with which to draw pictures.

Philip was afraid the man would come and try to find him, so he stayed locked in Astrid's house when she went to the store that morning. Astrid promised herself she would go into Oroville that weekend and talk to the welfare department. She would just enjoy the boy until then. He already looked better with food under his belt.

All afternoon Philip dipped his new goose feather in food coloring and drew pictures on the papers Astrid had given him. He drew a likeness of the man who had abducted him that was uncanny and when he put the feather on the table to get more paper, Astrid, fearful that it would fall off, picked it up. It was still warm; she held the feather against her cheek, yes it was really warm, like it was alive, probably because Philip had been holding it. Once again that evening the goose honked twice from the lake.

Day Four

Elmer left the house early to repair a roof in the area. Betty took an early bath then ate breakfast before she started to knit the sweater for her husband. Perhaps, just a little glass of sherry would perk her up before lunch and as she walked toward the liquor cabinet she thought of the lost feather. Oh well, maybe Elmer would bring her another. It was then she heard the goose honk, only once and quietly in the distance, but ignoring it she continued on her quest for the sherry. Just as she put her hand around the neck of the bottle, the goose honked a second time, but Betty didn't hear it. She poured herself a glass of wine and the room suddenly seemed to feel cold, so she used this as an excuse to drink the rest of the bottle. She got out her knitting. However her head was reeling and the stitches refused to stay on the needles so she curled up and went to sleep on the couch, and that was where Elmer found her when he came home.

*   *   *

Just after lunch Astrid borrowed the feather from Philip, promising she would bring him back a surprise from Oroville. Getting into her car she assured him she would be home before dinner. What she didn't say was that she planned to buy a cake and stick the feather in the frosting for a surprise. Astrid had never wanted children, but she loved them and her heart went out to this lost little boy.

She left Philip with a box of cookies, her colored pencils and plenty of paper, telling him she would return that afternoon, emphasizing, "Do not answer the door," which he promised not to do, crossing his heart to signify the promise, before he reached out to give her a hug.

On the road down to Orville with all the car windows open the feather flew off the front seat and landed on the highway behind her. Astrid, with her eyes on the road ahead, failed to notice that the feather was missing.

*   *   *

At Lake Madrone, Janet packed to leave the cabin, while Roger checked that all the doors and windows were locked before carrying their suitcases to the car. They hated to leave, but Roger had a faculty meeting in two days. Janet had packed a lunch to eat on the way, when she saw they were getting a late start.

About half way down the hill the traffic in both directions had stopped and when Roger looked, he saw a car had smashed into the mountainside. Two police cars and an ambulance were on the scene. Roger immediately recognized the car. Without a doubt the man being lifted on the stretcher from the car was the same smelly man who had been at their back door inquiring for his son. There was no one else in the smashed car. Janet had closed her eyes when she saw the accident or she might have seen a paramedic pick up a lone feather and tuck it under the body of the man on the stretcher, but she kept her hands over her face, eyes tightly closed until she heard Rodger speak, "Janet you can open your eyes now the ambulance is leaving."

My story ends after a flat tire caused the ambulance to careen over a steep embankment, triggering its rear doors to swing open and launch a dying man from a stretcher out onto a stony embankment There would be no green forest for him to roll towards and no lovely young girl to rescue him and cook him a warm meal. The killer in the clunker would journey to perdition, with his final breath accompanied only by a very cold feather.

Afterwards

In time, Philip's memory would metamorphose the feather into a ballpoint pen, sticking out of his very own chocolate cake given to him by his Aunt Astrid.

Only time will tell if Betty's contact with the feather left her with a large enough taste of sobriety to reshape her life with Elmer.

Roger and Jan were last seen vacationing in Scotland, hiking in the Highlands. Their lives would continue to be long, healthy, and happy.

Now you may ask about the goose? It would resurrect in another hundred years to fly over another lake to leave another warm feather somewhere in the world. I told you my story was magic!

The Journey

It was late afternoon, Sophia's husband Petar was working in the grape fields behind their house. Only an orange setting sun watched as Sophia crouched down under the Acacia tree in the front yard and felt the first gush of bloody amniotic fluid spurt onto the parched soil. Too late to reach the house, she bowed to the inevitable and when the sun had disappeared over the hills, the child was born. As the wind whipped through the branches overhead, she wrapped the infant in her underskirt and staggered from the yard up the path to her small wooden cottage. After climbing the three steps up to the front door, she called out for Petar.

When mother and child were comfortable in the bedroom, Petar sat beside her on the bed and without speaking, leaned over and kissed his wife gently on the forehead. No words passed between them. Outside the wind had stopped and inside the ticking of the wall clock was all to be heard.

Holding the infant to her breast, Sophia looked across into Petar's hazel eyes, studying his face before she spoke. "This baby will be called Sylvanus, the God of productive land, after the ancient Roman God of the lands, forests, fields and flocks."

Before replying, in an effort to hide his surprise, Petar looked down as he cupped his hand gently over the child's head.

"I will take him into my heart. We are truly honored to have Sylvanus." It was a name he had never heard before and he had to roll it through his mind and over his tongue a couple of times before he felt comfortable with it. When the child finished nursing, Sophia cradled him in the crook of her arm and lay back on the bed.

Petar, with his olive skin and dark hair, knew this baby, with skin as black as ebony, could not possibly be his. But with her complexion as white as milk, hair as yellow as corn silk, the child did not resemble Sophia either. He seemed to have his mother's blue eyes, but then all babies have bluish eyes at birth. In the heavens a crescent moon shown in an otherwise dark sky. Sophia reached out and put her warm hand on her husband's arm. He felt at peace with the world and Sophia knew he spoke the truth when he had said, "I will take him into my heart."

Outside under the acacia tree the amniotic fluid sparkled like fire as it slowly seeped into the rocky soil of Bosnia, but no one was there to notice.

Within the hour, there was a knock on the front door. Petar opened it to three young men, probably high school age, who politely requested water for their overheating car radiator. The tallest boy introduced himself as Miro, and his companions as Dusco and Sinisa and explained that his father owned a winery in Mostar. He went on to say they were on their way home from Medugorje when steam started coming out from under the hood of the car, forcing them to stop on the road. When Miro told Petar his father's name Petar recognized it at once, having sent grapes to him many times, and he cordially invited them inside while he brought them a large pitcher of water. When a tiny cry came from the other room Petar explained that not many hours ago a son had been born to his wife Sophia and all three boys joined in with congratulations. With many thanks the boys took the pitcher and walked down the three stairs and out to the car where they filled the radiator and Miro ran back with the pitcher. When Petar heard the car running he stepped outside and watched as its tail lights moved along the road like two red stars in the darkness.

When he returned to the bedroom Petar found Sylvanus sleeping soundly beside his mother, who lay wide-awake looking out into the darkness. After telling her about the three boys, there was a short silence before Petar, seeing something else was on her mind, took her hand.

"Petar, I was looking outside picturing Rimrods in the distance, their incandescent structures crawling slowly but surely to our part of the world." There was fear in her heart and tears in her eyes before she continued with the words, "Then what will happen to us?" Petar had no reply for her.

Turning her head, speaking more to the sleeping child than to her husband, she ran her fingers across the baby's cheek and continued, "I was also thinking of the natural beauty of the earth, you know, lovely places like Kravic Waterfalls, with pure water cascading down green mountainsides and even our healthy little vineyard with its plump red grapes. Then I thought of the sewage accumulating and piling up all over the world behind the Posner fences and fearing for…for well for all of us. The world's youth, like those boys you gave water to." Her voice drifted off. "But now I am so tired."

Petar looking at Sophia, wanting so badly to comfort her, but all that came to him to say was, "Sophia, you must be very tired, please try to rest now. Sylvanus is blessed to have you for his mother."

Perhaps she was asleep before she heard him, and again, perhaps not. The sliver of the moon in the eastern sky did little to brighten the darkness of the night.

*　　　*　　　*

The following day Petar and Sophia received a note with a package from Miro's father. The package contained a warm wooly baby blanket, a bottle of the finest blatina wine, and four little round loaves of Lepinja bread, soft, light, and still warm from the oven. The note was signed by the three boys, Miro, Dusko and Sinisa. Petar placed the gifts on the bed where Sophia and the child were sleeping, then kissed Sylvanus on the forehead before he tiptoed out of the room. The child must grow to maturity. It was important that the air be pure, the earth unadulterated, and the people, at least momentarily peaceful. Reckoned by the Christian calendar, the year was 1982. Sophia was 19 years old. They were in Europe in Bosnia Herzegovina on the Balkan Peninsula.

*　　　*　　　*

Sophia remembered the day her mother, Anna, lay dying in the hospital in Austria as she looked up and spoke to her only daughter for the last time.

"Sophia, your cousin Franz Buhler is a Parish priest at Medjugorje. You must go. He will know." But she didn't have the breath to finish. What will he know? It was too late for Sophia to ask.

After selling the household items from their modest flat in Carinthia, Austria, she paid the landlord for back rent and had enough to pay for her mother's burial. Finding herself, not only an orphan, but penniless at sixteen, she left school. The following day she left Austria for Bosnia Herzegovina. She had just enough money left for transportation to the parish of Medjugorje, the Shrine vying with Lourdes in France and Fatima in Portugal as one of the most frequently visited Catholic shrines in the world.

Walking into the village with one suitcase in her hand, she knocked at the door of the Presbytery. When a young Novice appeared and Sophia explained that she was Fr. Buhler's 16 year-old cousin from Austria the young boy invited her inside and went to find him. In what seemed like a matter of seconds a priest in a long black cassock appeared, introducing himself as Father Buhler. She looked at a man probably in his early or middle 30s. The priest, a little on the gaunt side, stood well over six feet and looked at her out of clear blue eyes, a quizzical expression on his face. Then he smiled and she noticed his teeth were somewhat crooked and badly stained, probably from tobacco. A deep cleft in the middle of his perfectly rounded chin gave him an almost handsome look. After reaching inside his cassock for his eyeglasses and adjusting them on his long nose, he stooped over a bit to get a closer look at his visitor. Her long straight golden hair, deep blue eyes and flawless white skin, almost transparent, reminded him of a Dresden doll, but he caught himself realizing this was no way to look at a young girl even if she was almost still a child: but somehow this 16-year-old girl did not seem like an ordinary child. Drawing his eyes away from her and his mind back to reality, he invited Sophia into the Presbytery, where they could sit and talk. After a short but painful discussion of her mother's last illness, Father Buhler patted her hand.

"Sophia child, we have a place for you here at least for a little while. What languages do you speak? I am thinking of the gift shop. Coming from Carinthia in Austria, I can hear you are fluent in Slovene, and German, how about French and English?" She hesitated just a bit before answering, "Well some English and petite French."

"Very good, we have many visitors from America, England, and France, but for now, let me show you the church and chapel" At the chapel they went inside to kneel before the Virgin and say a prayer for the souls of Sophia's mother and her father, Fr. Buhler's uncle, who had died in an automobile accident ten years ago.

Back outside Fr. Buhler suggested they stop for a bite to eat so they walked through the warm August winds, saturated with humidity from the Adriatic Sea, to the hall where food was being served to a group of tourists.

During their repast, her cousin told her about six young girls and two boys, receiving daily visitations from the Virgin Mary, with messages to pray for world peace. Almost from the time of the first visitation in 1981, it had been a financial boom to the parish and the church was profiting greatly. She listened without comment. Just then, eight young people walked by the table and Fr. Buhler stopped them and introduced them as the young visionaries. After acknowledging the introductions, Sophia's hands turned icy cold, even though the afternoon sun shone directly on them through the window. A momentary dizziness seemed to grip her, but she managed a weak smile and a nod as the visionaries walked away. Perhaps it was just her intake of so much food after the two day fast.

When lunch was finished, she accompanied Fr. Buhler as he showed her the church, chapel, and Apparition Hill where prayers are said three times a week. But seeing she was getting tired, he took her to the Mother's Village, a shelter offered to unwed destitute and homeless mothers as well as other needy women. Once in bed she was too tired to let anything disturb her sleep.

That same night on the other side of the parish, this priest was not finding sleep as easily as Sophia had. He thought of the words Marita had spoken before Sophia had arrived that morning in the St. Francis garden. The young gypsy girl had tapped him lightly on his arm, diverting his eyes from a little lame boy being led around the garden on a pony. When the priest saw the worried look on her face he took Marita's hand and led her to an isolated bench under an apple tree where they sat side-by-side. It didn't seem like 10 years ago that this pretty almond skinned, black-eyed little Roma had been brought to Medjugorje after the roadside found her abandoned, cold, and hungry. She had moved into the Mother's Village and learned to read and write with Fr. Buhler as her mentor. Now, when she said she had something to tell him and he saw her serious expression, he was concerned.

"Yes my child?" Then he sat back as she began to speak. He was looking in the distance when she started but within seconds her words got his full attention. When she finished speaking they both stood up. It was just at that moment that he got the message that his cousin was at Medjugorje. He soon learned it was Sophia. He had not seen her since she was a baby.

That night Franz Buhler couldn't help but think about Marita as he walked toward the Presbytery after evening mass. He knew that Gypsies were still roaming Bosnia and selling pagan edicts and predictions peppered with black magic. However, Marita had never known any Gypsies, or Roma as they were called, and given her Catholic education, should not have had pagan thoughts about predicting the future. Might she be referring to an apparition of the blessed mother? But somehow that just didn't fit, not the way she had phrased it.

In bed that night, his thoughts went back to his childhood, to a father he had never seen, who had left his Catholic wife and infant son in Austria, returning to Israel just weeks after Franz was born and had not been heard of since. Franz had always wondered about his Jewish father. His mother had only spoken of him only as Abraham the Hasidic. Then, his thoughts returned to Marita the little gypsy, who would probably never know her mother or her father either. Then, was it a coincidence that his beautiful young cousin appeared the same day Marita had spoken to him? These thoughts bounced around inside his brain like soap bubbles. He turned over to try to sleep on his other side but sleep didn't come until almost dawn. Why did my father not stay in Austria to become a Christian, where was he now? Who really knows our destinies or where we are headed. Who are God's chosen? And again, are there many Gods? Marita's words spoken yesterday were etched in his mind.

"Father you must know this. There is a woman coming here who will be truly blessed by all the Gods. I have seen her in the stars."

*   *   *

For a year, Sophia had been working in the souvenir shop by day and helping at night in the Mother's Village, a specialized haven for abandoned or neglected children, unwed mothers and the elderly. Everyone was so nice. Her doubts, as to the authenticity of the young visionaries seemed to come in unfinished, but disturbing reflections. She never spoke with the young visionaries, in fact she avoided them and avoided talking to her cousin about them. She always made her confessions to another priest. To say she was happy might be too much, but to say she was contented seemed quite enough. By not allowing any doubts to surface, she was able to mollify her thoughts, even convince herself it was no affair of hers. And who was to say it was not God's will so that prosperity would reign in this Holy Church? It was certainly drawing a crowd from all over the world.

Sophia stood behind the counter arranging religious items for sale in the showcase beneath the glass counter, when a young farmer came to request one of their rosaries, the one fashioned from thorns unique to the region. As Sophia handed him the brown beads, their hands met. Fr. Buhler, watching from the doorway was smiling and thinking—Petar is a fine young Serbian, yes indeed, he would make a good husband for Sophia. Before the sale was terminated, the two young people had agreed to meet again and six months later they married.

After a quiet ceremony in the Adoration Chapel the couple moved to Petar's farm in the tiny village of Miletina, a rural area in the parish of Medjugorje, near the larger towns in Bosnia. Sophia, wrapped in burka-like clothing to protect her fair skin from the sun, worked side-by-side in the vineyard with Petar. It was arduous work tending the vines in such rocky soil under the hot sun, but the Zilavka wine brought in a modest income from the red grapes, which grew particularly plump in this area. Pomegranate and fig trees also graced the property, but brought little or no money. Chickens and a few pigs, and an ample vegetable garden completed the picture of this small self-sufficient farm. Petar, an only son, had inherited the farm the same year he married Sophia.

*   *   *

After Sylvanus was born, Petar built a grape arbor attached to the back of the house. Soon it was covered with vines. In the spring, the sweet smell of the hanging clusters of grapes permeated the air. Petar, a skilled carpenter, built a table and benches for the family and weather permitting, they ate outside.

Sylvanus, like the grapevines on the arbor, grew rapidly. His parents had furnished him with an arbor of love to support his healthy bones and good health. His body was straight and strong and from the time he was little he liked to handle a hoe and cultivate the vineyard. It was August, and the grapes were ready to be harvested. Sophia and Petar needed protection from the rays of the sun as they worked in the early morning or late afternoon, but Sylvanus would go without a hat, stripped to the waist and work the whole day without so much as a sign of a sunburn.

One afternoon when Sophia appeared at the doorway with a plate of cheese and homemade sauerkraut, Petar walked in and turned to her with concern. "Sylvanus is out under the Acacia tree telling stories to the children again. I only heard a word as I went by, but he said something about talking to God in the sun. Now really Sophia, I don't think your cousin would care for that." Sophia placed the cheese down on the table and thought for moment before answering.

"Petar, the most important thing is that the children liked the story. After all, Sylvanus is only ten-years-old and Father Buhler didn't hear him. It is frightening though, the things that come out of that child's mouth. Questions about the sun and the stars— just yesterday he asked me if I knew how big and how far away the moon was. He asks things like why is the sun so orange every evening, and what are the stars made of? Or why his skin is dark?"

Petar just shook his head. He, too, had wondered about the boy's dark skin, but now he just helped himself to a piece cheese and Sophia took little heed as she continued, "He asked me why he never felt cold when the other children in school needed a sweater or when the cold wind blew ferociously he could still walk about without a coat. Petar I just don't know."

*   *   *

Less than a century ago, the late Dr. Jacob Posner, a young Israeli genius in mechanical engineering, designed, created and developed mobile fencing, now manufactured internationally under the name of Posner's Rimrods Inc. These Rimrods came in flexible sections, indestructible synthetic metal, held together with hollow posts, extending either horizontally or vertically; automated by nuclear power to seek out, then enclose and thus isolate the planets' growing waste; metals, plastics, broken machinery, and obsolete technology. Soon these designated dumpsites generated lethal chemical soups, emitted deadly vapors, absorbed radiation and contributed to a dangerous rise in the world's temperature. Across the earth, areas of non-biodegradable excrement, better known as toxic waste, piled up. Most of humanity saw these fences as their salvation for enclosing their unwanted contaminates.

The income generated from the sale of these creeping fences, like the revenue from coal and oil, was soon under the control of immense cartels, entrepreneurs, and politicians. Moguls growing rich were able to convince the media to downplay and even deny much of the health hazards from acerbic soups of chemical waste, simmering on earth's manmade burners and endangering life. Posner Rimrod's stock soared.

What would happen when the Posner fences had nothing to do but meet themselves traveling around the earth? Humans had tried, but could not survive for any length of time behind the Rimrods and those who dared soon sickened and died. Sylvanus would be 13 when Rimrods were first seen in Bosnia on the distant Dalmatian Coast.

*   *   *

Four years of war freed Bosnia from the Socialist regime. Sylvanus, too young to fight, remained at home going to school and working in the vineyard until he left home to attend the University of Sarajevo where he graduated with honors four years later. Petar and Sophia attended his graduation, as did Fr. Buhler.

It was the day after the graduation ceremony from Sarajevo University, that Sylvanus, Petar, Sophia and Fr. Buhler walked to one of the little coffeehouses just outside the campus. They were seated in a booth along the side wall just a few steps from the front door when two ragged children pushed open the door and stood looking at the table; gypsy children probably no more than 10 years-old with stringy greasy hair dressed in dirty ill-fitting clothing. Gypsy children were prevalent in the area most probably coming from Ciljuge, a home to many gypsies, about 45 miles north of Sarajevo. The Roma lived there in abject poverty, often in cardboard boxes set up as living quarters without electricity, water or heat. They supported their humble lifestyle by begging, telling fortunes and scrounging, stealing, and selling what little scrap iron they could find. The owner of the coffee shop always tried his best to bar them from entering but he was nowhere to be seen. The gypsy children were soon joined by a shabbily dressed gypsy woman in a long skirt with a dirty red and green shawl wrapped round her head, and blood-red beads around her neck. The woman stopped halfway across the room and bowed low to Sophia saying something indiscernible to one of the children before she approached the table and spoke directly to Sophia. "Dear lady, you are truly blessed by all the gods. I have seen you in the stars."

Sophia looked at her with pity as the thought flashed across her mind that, had things been different she might have been the one begging for her bread and butter. Reaching in her purse she took out a Marka and laid it on the table and smiled at the woman. The gypsy nodded back and without further ado picked up the coin and put it in her pocket, just moments before the owner of the café, a pudgy little Serbian, came running over and shooed all the Romas outside. Sophia rose to protest but Sylvanus put his arm around her and suggested she just sit quietly. Fr. Buhler looked into his coffee cup, his face grey when he heard the words of the gypsy.

*   *   *

Back home again in her kitchen Sophia was stirring the sauerkraut on the stove as she turned to Petar, who was drinking a glass of goat's milk and munching on a single cookie. He had put on considerable weight in the 20 years since Sylvanus had been born, but she took it as a compliment to her good cooking, learned from her mother. It was good to have Sylvanus home from the university, even for three months. She was proud of the scholarship he had earned and would miss him when he returned to Sarajevo to work toward a Masters in astrophysics, but for now he was having a well-deserved rest. Sophia, still holding the spoon in her hand looked at her husband.

"Petar have you seen Sylvanus?"

"Where else? Look under the Acacia tree in the front. I swear that child is a natural born teacher."

Wiping her hands on her apron, the universal sign of a woman exiting her kitchen, she walked out the front door. Sylvanus was perched on a kitchen stool with five or six now nearly grown children sitting at his feet.

Sophia, thinking this might be an annoyance to the children, quietly asked him if he would like to have lunch now. His light blue eyes twinkled with kindness as he thought how fleeting a lifetime could be, before he answered, "Childhood is a stamp of belonging. Childhood unites all mankind. There is no man alive in this war-torn world that hasn't once been a child." Then looking at Sophia he realized her hair had turned grey and there were little age lines around her eyes, so he assured her he would come in very soon.

After finishing the story and saying good-by to the visitors he returned to the house and he and his mother had a glass of red wine together before lunch. The sun seemed to shine a little brighter.

*   *   *

Throughout the years Sylvanus had always began his stories to the children with:

In the beginning many, many years ago the sun created man and woman from the materials here on the earth.

He molded the wet clay into human forms and left them in his sunshine to harden, or as we say these days, to grow up. He let them learn right from wrong as they hardened into their permanent shapes, or as we say these days, became adults. Every morning he shone on them from one side of the world and every evening he said goodnight from the other.

The children would then add to this story with innovations from their own thoughts. Sylvanus called this the 'What if game.' He loved spinning stories of the clay people, their wanderings over the earth—the messages from the Sun God, the wind and the stars. Youngsters never failed to feel they were part of every story as they sat discussing their decisions and choices and adding to a story. But that was many years ago and today those children were no longer children.

By now the original 'What if game' players, who had gathered by his feet years ago, were young adults, living on what is considered the safe side of the Posner Fences. Most of the people in the world paid little more heed to the creeping fences, as anything but a necessity for their comfort. Like giant restrooms for waste you just junked things of no use behind the fence. Nobody wants to fight for the job of cleaning up contaminated waste, so things piled up where they landed, as the fences inched forward to make more room for more waste.

In Sylvanus's part of the world Muslims and Bosnians fought and died for political power, and what they considered God-given territorial rights for the very land now so toxic that neither man nor beast could exist there. Toxicity was slowly spreading in The Americas, Asia, Europe, at the same time as the population was declining as a grey haze settled over two thirds of the world.

One night after a particularly beautiful sunset, air pollution will cause this phenomenon—Sylvanus composed a letter to the General Assembly at the United Nations in New York, enclosing an article he had written in the Sarajevo University Newsletter. He mailed it to America.

*   *   *

It was midsummer when a letter came from the United States, inviting him, his way paid, to visit America and share in a round table discussion with young honorary students at the General Assembly of the United Nations. It mentioned the Posner Rimrods, the article published in the Sarajevo University Newspaper, just before he graduated, emphasizing the immediate need for alternative earth friendly ways to convert and reuse the refuge of a technological world. Eleven other nations had also been invited to participate in a discussion of greenhouse gasses and the pros and cons of global warming. The Assembly would meet in one month. When Sylvanus received the reply he was ecstatic and after reading it out loud looked at Peter and Sophia, "Can you believe it? I am going to take part in a 'What if game' in the United States."

Sophia didn't smile as he had expected, but said instead, "Sylvanus what if you didn't go?"

He shut his eyes and answered, "Mother you know I must."

And all she said was, "I know son."

A month later Petar and Sophia waved their good-bye's from the doorway of their home in Bosnia and Sylvanus, his backpack on his back, rode his bicycle the three miles to the airport.

The morning of first day of the conference some of the finest young scientific minds in the world gathered in America outside, under the world flags at the United Nations building in New York. A young man from Bosnia stood at the back of the group, escaping with his life when an errant child, riding a bicycle knocked him into an adjoining alley just before an assassin set off a suicide bomb, turning the remaining people on the street into a bloody carnage. In the confusion that followed, the lone Bosnian walked away undetected, down the dark alley, and next day left New York by freighter, disguised as a tourist from Africa. Headlines in the New York Times read, outside the United Nations building in New York. Terrorists set off a car bomb killing all those on the street.

*   *   *

Traveling as an Ethiopian, Sylvanus made his way back to the vineyard in Militena. When he arrived home, he knelt under the Acacia tree and looked up through the branches and when the hot sun reached its zenith he lowered his head.

"Forgive them Father, for this time they know not what they need to do" His head still bowed he heard the wind softly whisper a message for his ears alone.

Entering the house he greeted Sophia and Petar who jumped up from their chairs in joyous relief when they saw him alive. After kissing each on both cheeks, he assured them three times in a row that he was safe. The phone rang in the living room and Petar rose to answer it, leaving Sylvanus alone with Sophia.

"Mother, we must soon leave. You must come with me." Then seeing the look on her face as she looked toward the living room he took her hand and guided her out under the grape arbor.

With sadness, he looked at her graying hair and worry-lined face.

"You are truly blessed among women but we..." At that moment, a roar like a tidal wave came forth from the sky, blotting out any further words, and at the same instant the earth grew dark and in the next second there was a giant explosion. Neither mother nor son heard the noise for just nanoseconds before the blast, still holding hands, they had transmuted into vapor.

*   *   *

The Sun watched this massive explosion. Fires on Earth's surface and molten lava from its core spewed forth burning animal, vegetable and mineral in every direction, peppered with pieces of Posner's Rimrods. Earths elliptical orbit around the Sun would now hold the fragments of a once animated planet mixed with pieces of a famous indestructible fence.

Robert Oppenheimer, a nuclear physicist born in America and Jacob Posner, a mechanical engineer born in Israel, would never meet. Oppenheimer built the atomic bomb, a swift and deadly radioactive bomb, giving man the ability and the choice to destroy all life on the planet. Posner built the Rimrod Fences, creeping, menacing mobile enclosures, capable of containing toxic dumpsites until their contents grew larger than these containers could handle.

*   *   *

However, it was neither toxins, famine, fences nor an atomic bomb that ended life on earth—but an asteroid. In fact, the Sun had sent the asteroid earthbound as an act of mercy to save mankind from what would be an excruciatingly hideous death on the path it had chosen. If only human beings could have paid attention and joined together to heed the warning signs of self-destruction this would not have been necessary.

*   *   *

On an unnamed planet in space, where time was reckoned neither forward nor backward, children sat on the soft mossy ground under a blossoming Acacia tree, their shiny black faces looking up at their teacher. They never seemed to tire of hearing his story that always began… "In the beginning, when our planet was young, before the land was cultivated and forests flourished,

197

animals ran in great herds and your distant sun created man from vapor."

One little boy with sky blue eyes looked at the teacher, raised his hand and asked, "Sylvanus, can we play the 'What if game' now? Please?"